NIPHER MIDDLE SCHOOL
700 SOUTH KIRKWOOD ROAD
KIRKWOOD, MISSOURI 63122 DEMCO

ECSTASY

by Stephanie Lane

**DRUG
EDUCATION
LIBRARY**

LUCENT BOOKS

An imprint of Thomson Gale, a part of The Thomson Corporation

Detroit • New York • San Francisco • San Diego • New Haven, Conn.
Waterville, Maine • London • Munich

LIBRARY OF CONGRESS CATALOGING-IN-PUBLICATION DATA

Lane, Stephanie, 1975–
    Ecstasy / by Stephanie Lane.
        p. cm. — (Drug education library)
    Includes bibliographical references and index.
    ISBN 1-59018-415-7 (hbk. : alk. paper)
    1. Ecstasy (Drug)—Juvenile literature. I. Title. II. Series.
RM666.M35L36 2005
615'.7883--dc22

2004013440

Printed in the United States of America

Contents

Foreword

The development of drugs and drug use in America is a cultural paradox. On the one hand, strong, potentially dangerous drugs provide people with relief from numerous physical and psychological ailments. Sedatives like Valium counter the effects of anxiety; steroids treat severe burns, anemia, and some forms of cancer; morphine provides quick pain relief. On the other hand, many drugs (sedatives, steroids, and morphine among them) are consistently misused or abused. Millions of Americans struggle each year with drug addictions that overpower their ability to think and act rationally. Researchers often link drug abuse to criminal activity, traffic accidents, domestic violence, and suicide.

These harmful effects seem obvious today. Newspaper articles, medical papers, and scientific studies have highlighted the myriad problems drugs and drug use can cause. Yet, there was a time when many of the drugs now known to be harmful were actually believed to be beneficial. Cocaine, for example, was once hailed as a great cure, used to treat everything from nausea and weakness to colds and asthma. Developed in Europe during the 1880s, cocaine spread quickly to the United States where manufacturers made it the primary ingredient in such everyday substances as cough medicines, lozenges, and tonics. Likewise, heroin, an opium derivative, became a popular painkiller during the late nineteenth century. Doctors and patients flocked to American drugstores to buy heroin, described as the optimal cure for even the worst coughs and chest pains.

As more people began using these drugs, though, doctors, legislators, and the public at large began to realize that they were more damaging than beneficial. After years of using heroin as a painkiller, for example, patients began asking their doctors for larger and stronger doses. Cocaine users reported dangerous side effects, including hallucinations and wild mood shifts. As a result, the U.S. government initiated more stringent regulation of many powerful and addictive drugs, and in some cases outlawed them entirely.

A drug's legal status is not always indicative of how dangerous it is, however. Some drugs known to have harmful effects can be purchased legally in the United States and elsewhere. Nicotine, a key ingredient in cigarettes, is known to be highly addictive. In an effort to meet their bodies' demands for nicotine, smokers expose themselves to lung cancer, emphysema, and other life-threatening conditions. Despite these risks, nicotine is legal almost everywhere.

Other drugs that cannot be purchased or sold legally are the subject of much debate regarding their effects on physical and mental health. Marijuana, sometimes described as a gateway drug that leads users to other drugs, cannot legally be used, grown, or sold in this country. However, some research suggests that marijuana is neither addictive nor a gateway drug and that it might actually benefit cancer and AIDS patients by reducing pain and encouraging failing appetites. Despite these findings and occasional legislative attempts to change the drug's status, marijuana remains illegal.

The Drug Education Library examines the paradox of drugs and drug use in America by focusing on some of the most commonly used and abused drugs or categories of drugs available today. By discussing objectively the many types of drugs, their intended purposes, their effects (both planned and unplanned), and the controversies surrounding them, the books in this series provide readers with an understanding of the complex role drugs and drug use play in American society. Informative sidebars, annotated bibliographies, and organizations to contact lists highlight the text and provide young readers with many opportunities for further discussion and research.

▉ Introduction

A Growing Problem

Few drugs in recent history have become quite so popular so fast as the designer drug known as ecstasy, officially known by its chemical name, 3, 4-methylenedioxymethamphetamine (MDMA). Indeed, statistics show that ecstasy use among all high school students is alarmingly high. The Monitoring the Future study, a leading annual survey of teenage drug use conducted by the University of Michigan, found that in 1997 3.5 percent of twelfth-graders had used ecstasy. In 2000 that figure more than doubled to 8 percent and in 2004 it had dropped to a little over 4 percent.

Part of ecstasy's popularity may stem from a widely held perception that its dangers are less extreme than those associated with other illegal drugs. In fact, deaths directly attributable to taking ecstasy are rare. The side effects most often observed include depression after the drug wears off, panic attacks, and in extreme cases, psychological addiction. Ecstasy users do seem able to function normally on a day-to-day basis, holding down jobs and maintaining relationships, for example, and those who stop using the drug appear not to experience withdrawal symptoms. Some experts caution, however, that there is ample anecdotal evidence that ecstacy is not as harmless as some would like to believe. "There's a notion that ecstasy makes you feel good, that there's no downside," U.S. Customs commissioner Raymond Kelly, whose agency frequently intercepts shipments of illegal drugs, including ecstasy, told *Time* magazine. "But there's plenty of horror stories."[1]

Despite ecstasy's reputation as a relatively benign drug, experts in the field of drug research say that what worries them most about ecstasy's exploding popularity is that it is taking place in the absence of concrete information. These experts caution, for example, that little is known about the drug's long-term effects including possibly permanent changes in brain chemistry. Yet even this hypothesis is questionable, since it comes from studying addicts who use large doses of ecstasy in addition to other drugs. Under such circumstances, researchers have no way of

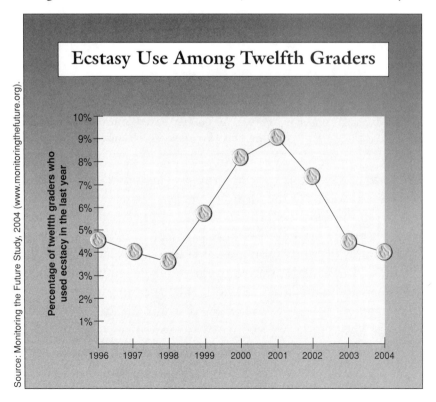

Source: Monitoring the Future Study, 2004 (www.monitoringthefuture.org).

A teen displays a tablet of ecstasy on his tongue. Recent statistics show that ecstasy use among high school students has fallen off in the last few years.

being certain how much of the drug is being taken, nor can they verify the absence of other drugs in the user's system.

Still, studies involving rhesus monkey subjects suggest to the nation's policy makers that there is reason for concern. These studies imply that long-term use does cause permanent damage to the brain. Particularly affected in the monkeys studied was their brains' ability to manufacture and regulate certain chemicals vital to controlling mood and sleep. Furthermore, research done on humans who use ecstasy frequently suggests that over time, the drug erodes short-term memory.

Other experts see the risks as more immediate. "We are dancing with danger here, because kids and their parents think of ecstasy as a benign party drug," Michelle Leonhart, a special agent from the Los Angeles office of the federal Drug Enforcement Administration (DEA), told a reporter for *The New York Times*. "They don't see what we see, that it's a neurotoxin with serious side effects, that people die from overdoses."[2]

Just how dangerous ecstasy is remains a hot issue in the scientific community, where researchers seem to fall into strict pro-ecstasy or anti-ecstasy camps. Those who argue that the drug is dangerous tend to characterize these dangers as extreme. Other scientists argue that the drug's dangers have been exaggerated, and that at the very least some research into potential therapeutic use of the drug is justified. What most scientists do agree on is that the continuing use of this powerful drug among America's youth means that more research is needed.

Chapter 1

Ecstasy Arrives

The chemical compound today called ecstasy was known to scientists early in the twentieth century, but was not ingested by humans until 1976. At that time, however, ecstasy was not used outside a medical setting. Psychiatrists, looking for ways to speed the course of psychotherapy, administered it to their patients. These psychiatrists thought that because ecstasy—or MDMA, as it was then known—was chemically similar to a family of drugs called entactogens (literally, "to touch within," so called because they seemed to aid people in becoming more introspective), it might help their patients bring to the surface deeply repressed and painful memories.

Classification

In addition to being classified as an entactogen, ecstasy fits into a category known as designer drugs. Unlike drugs such as marijuana or cocaine, both of which are derived from plants, designer drugs are manufactured, usually in small garage- or kitchen-based labs. Those who make drugs in this way sometimes incorporate more than one drug into the mixture, creating a substance that falls into two or more drug classes. For example, ecstasy contains mescaline, a hallucinogen, and amphetamine, a stimulant. Hallucinogens produce distortions in users' perceptions of the world around them as well as visual or auditory hallucinations. Stimulants raise heart rate and have an energizing effect. Both of these effects can be seen in the high that ecstasy produces.

In addition to its hallucinogenic and stimulative properties, ecstasy creates a sensation in the user of being connected to other people and self-aware, as though he or she has reached, or has access to, some part of the mind that was previously inaccessible.

Appearance and Dosage

Although pure ecstasy is a white powder, the drug is most commonly found in pill form. The appearance of ecstasy pills varies widely. They come in various colors and are often stamped with pictures (such as flowers or butterflies), characters (such as Pokemon) from popular culture, words (like *sex* or *truth*), or logos

These are all pills of MDMA, better known as ecstasy. Although popular today as a recreational drug, ecstasy was first used in the 1970s by psychiatrists as a therapeutic aid.

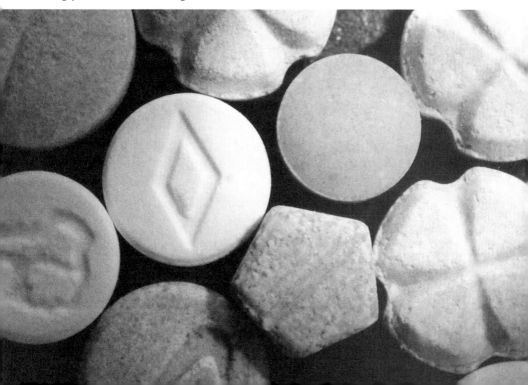

from products that are popular among young people. Dealers use these stamps or symbols to "brand" their pills and set them apart from others. In a culture in which brands and the images associated with them are important, the use of such logos may affect individuals' decisions as to which ecstasy pill to buy, even though the actual chemical characteristics are identical.

Though ecstasy is most often found in pill form, it can also be snorted, smoked, or ingested anally. However it is ingested, a normal dose of ecstasy is generally considered to be 100–125 milligrams. Users report that they feel the first effects of ecstasy after twenty to forty minutes; the drug's peak effect occurs about sixty to ninety minutes after ingestion.

Creation

Although ecstasy is known to stimulate feelings of connection to others, it was not created with that quality in mind. The drug was discovered in 1912 by the German pharmaceutical company Merck as a by-product in the synthesis of a medication, called hydrastinin, that was used to stop bleeding. As is common industry practice, the company patented what at the time was called MDMA, even though it was not intended for medical use.

MDMA was largely ignored for nearly six decades. Between 1914 and 1970, ecstasy was resynthesized and studied only once. In 1953 military researchers at the Army Chemical Center in Maryland studied MDMA along with seven other drugs that because of their chemical structure were thought likely to have powerful psychoactive effects. In particular, MDMA was thought to have potential for use in "brainwashing"—that is, to erase longheld beliefs and replace them with others. MDMA was administered to rats, mice, guinea pigs, dogs, and monkeys to test its toxicity and behavioral effects. But MDMA was never adopted for use by the military, and the drug faded into obscurity again.

Alexander Shulgin

The obscurity continued throughout the 1960s and into the 1970s. Although hallucinogens such as LSD, psilocybin, and mescaline were considered for possible use in psychotherapy, ecstasy was not, despite its known psychoactive properties.

Then in 1976 a biochemist named Alexander Shulgin heard about ecstasy. Shulgin was an enthusiastic proponent of psychedelic drugs. He had synthesized a number of drugs in his home laboratory, taken the drugs himself, and occasionally given them to friends as well. Shulgin had published accounts of his experiments in various scientific journals, but work with psychedelics was still just a sideline for him. Eventually Shulgin got the chance to concentrate on psychedelics. As part of his work with Dow Chemical Company, Shulgin created one of the world's first biodegradable insecticides, Zectran. As a reward for that discovery, Dow gave him a generous payment for the patent and unlimited freedom to pursue whatever subject interested him.

"I've always been interested in the machinery of the mental process," Shulgin recalled in an interview with the *New York Times*. "I'm curious!"[3] His interest in psychedelics stemmed from his first experience with mescaline in 1960, during which he spent the afternoon completely fascinated by his surroundings, and recognized the power of hallucinogens to bring to the surface otherwise inaccessible memories and experiences. Of that afternoon, he says:

> [Everything I experienced] had been brought about by a fraction of a gram of a white solid, but . . . in no way whatsoever could it be argued that these memories had been contained within the white solid. . . . I understood that our entire universe is contained in the mind and the spirit. We may choose not to find access to it, we may even deny its existence, but it is indeed there inside us, and there are chemicals that can catalyze its availability.[4]

Rediscovering MDMA

Shulgin's experiments with MDMA began in 1976, when a former student of his prompted him to attempt to resynthesize MDMA. Although Shulgin cannot recall how that individual knew about the drug, he remembers trying ecstasy himself and not being impressed by the drug's hallucinogenic effects. He compared the effects to an unusually lucid alcohol buzz, claiming, "It didn't have the other visual and auditory imaginative things that

In 1976 biochemist Alexander Shulgin began researching the psychotherapeutic effects of ecstasy. His work helped to convince many psychiatrists of the drug's clinical value.

you often get from psychedelics. It opened up a person, both to other people and inner thoughts, but didn't necessarily color it with pretty colors and strange noises."[5] Still he thought the drug's ability to "open up a person" might make MDMA well-suited to psychotherapy.

Shulgin often shared his chemical creations with a group of eight friends that he dubbed "the research group." One of these friends was a retired psychotherapist named Leo Zeff. After trying MDMA himself, Zeff, who was an ardent supporter of the use of hallucinogens in psychotherapy, was so favorably impressed that he urged fellow practitioners to administer the drug to their patients.

Zeff and his colleagues believed that ecstasy had the potential to aid psychotherapy in two ways: by lowering the defenses of patients and by making them feel closer to their psychotherapist. The psychotherapists who experimented with the drug appreciated the drug's ability to calm their clients and give them the ability to discuss traumatic issues. These were informal studies, not rigorous trials carried out in controlled settings. Still, the drug became quite popular with a select group of psychotherapists. These doctors referred to the drug as "Adam," because it appeared to induce in patients a blissful and innocent state that the doctors associated with the biblical story of Adam in the Garden of Eden.

Eventually, in 1978 Shulgin published the first scientific paper on ecstasy use by humans. In it he stated that ecstasy produced "an easily controlled altered state of consciousness with emotional and sensual overtones."[6] Bouyed by Shulgin's report, psychotherapists began treating certain patients with MDMA and continued to do so throughout the late 1970s and early 1980s.

The Godfather of MDMA on Rave Culture

In her book *Ecstasy: The Complete Guide,* Julie Holland asks Alexander Shulgin, the man who published the first paper about MDMA in the 1970s and is largely responsible for its popularity among psychotherapists at that time, about rave culture. He explained that going to raves is a form of rebellion for youth:

My feeling about the rave culture is that it is a representation of an inevitable form of behavior of people who are coming into adolescence and young adulthood. It's a way of becoming an independent person—not having to answer to authority, to parents, and establishing oneself as an individual. In that age group of fifteen to twenty-five years, you are immortal, and you don't care for the older generation. As the old saying goes, "Don't trust anyone over thirty." And I don't think it is unique to the rave community; it is specific to that stage of development. Everyone through the entire history of human beings has experienced that same rebellion against authority. It happened to express itself in this generation as rave culture, but in another, it might be jazz music at Golden Gate Park.

Therapeutic Use in the 1970s and 1980s

Even before Shulgin's report was published, a number of psychiatrists had concluded that the drug might enhance or speed up psychotherapy. Richard Doblin, a doctoral student at Harvard University, claims that "between 1977 and 1985, roughly half a million doses were administered for the treatment of depression, anxiety, rape-related trauma, and even schizophrenia."[7]

Anecdotal accounts suggest that psychotherapists were very pleased with MDMA's effects on their patients. Many psychotherapists recounted examples of their patients reaching breakthroughs in treatment—breakthroughs that normally took months of weekly sessions in traditional psychotherapy—after only one MDMA-assisted session. George Greer, a psychiatrist who administered MDMA to eighty patients during the 1980s, claims, "Without exception, every therapist who I talked to or even heard of, every therapist who gave MDMA to a patient, was highly impressed by the results."[8] Despite MDMA's frequent use as a psychotherapeutic aid at this time, the practitioners themselves largely kept quiet about such treatments. They worried that if word of the potency of MDMA became widely known, the government might ban its use—something that had already happened with another powerful psychoactive drug, LSD.

The Ecstasy Experience

Because psychotherapists chose to keep their experiments with MDMA under wraps, there are no official, scientifically verified accounts of patients' experiences with the drug. Most of what is known of ecstasy's effects comes from reports by individuals who have tried it in the relatively uncontrolled environment of a dance club or other public gathering. These effects, however, are widely known and more or less consistent.

Users report that when they take ecstasy, the effects of the drug come on quickly. Some find these effects—at least initially—pleasurable. Journalist Dawn MacKeen, in the online magazine Salon.com, describes the early stage of an ecstasy high, known as the "rush":

> It's been less than an hour, and you can already feel it. The corners of your mouth are starting to lift up, creating a big semicircle, a Cheshire grin.

The pit of your stomach, normally so weighed down with stress, is lightening. You're giddy, like the first time you fell for someone. The pupils of your eyes are dilating, growing with excitement. You look around and announce to the world that you're in love—with everyone and everything. Suddenly a new feeling hits; you realize it's all been [practice] until this instant, a slow buildup of excitement that you couldn't stop. But now, before you realize it, before you can control it, it's here. You want to let out a scream; you are so . . . happy. It's like the best moment in your life.[9]

At the same time, some users find the intensity of emotions frightening. A twenty-two-year-old graduate student recalls experiencing a sense of emotional overload during his first experience with ecstasy, describing it as, "'Oh, too much!' You know . . . that on-edge feeling like, 'Oh, I'm just about ready to explode!'"[10] After a few minutes (the time lag can vary from only ten minutes to almost an hour), this rush seems to be followed by a more steady "plateau phase," in which the intensity diminishes and the user calms down. Researchers Jerome Back and Marsha Rosenbaum, in their book *Pursuit of Ecstasy: The MDMA Experience*, describe

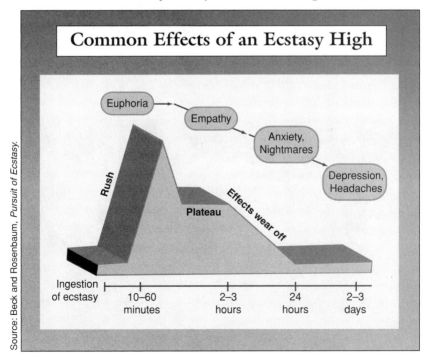

Source: Beck and Rosenbaum, *Pursuit of Ecstasy*.

the contrast between the rush and plateau phase: "For a few users (particularly novices), the transition to this more comfortable state of being came as a welcome relief to the anxiety experienced during the initial rush. . . . This 'plateau' phase generally lasts from two to three hours."[11] All told, the rush and plateau stages last roughly four hours, after which the drug's effects wear off.

Empathy

Of the various effects reported by users of ecstasy, one of the most common is a sense of empathy, an unaccustomed sense of understanding and feeling close to others. In his book *Ecstasy: The MDMA Story*, Bruce Eisner defines empathy as "projecting our imagination outside of ourselves and into another human being."[12] Some users report that feeling empathy allows them to forgive people who have wronged them in some way. For example, Jennie, a twenty-year-old college student, reported that after using ecstasy, she began to forgive her father for mentally and physically abusing her.

At the same time that the drug brings on a sense of empathy, it also tends to reduce the user's own worries about his or her imper-

Ecstasy elicits a strong feeling of empathy in users, causing them to feel intimately close to those around them.

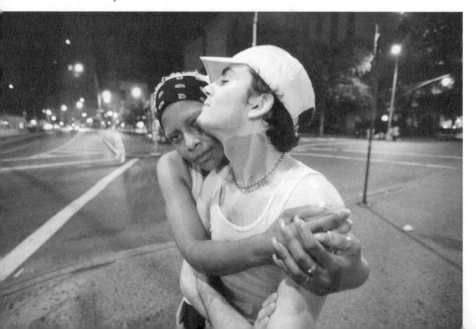

fections. Writer Matthew Klam discusses this effect of ecstasy: "[We let] go of . . . humiliation and awkwardness. This was the beginning of a long night of feeling uncharacteristically undefensive, comfortable and kind." He goes on to say of his own first-time experience with the drug, "And: all afternoon, all night, I didn't hate myself."[13] This enhanced sense of self-acceptance can lead users to open up and say what is on their minds. One user explains:

> I believe it lowers your sense of fear and you fall in love with yourself. When you do that, you're more willing to take risks, and one of the risks is telling the truth. In that sense, it's a truth drug. You feel like telling the truth. You feel like being honest. And you know you can say even some very delicate things without hurting people, and therefore you can speak the truth.

This does not mean, the user continues, that what someone says under the influence of ecstasy is necessarily true: "On the other hand, I would say . . . you can tell lies. You can withhold the truth if you need to. You're not *forced* to tell the truth."[14]

How Ecstasy Works

What virtually every user of ecstasy reports experiencing is euphoria, which is the result of changes in the chemistry of the brain. According to Alan Leshner, the director of the National Institute on Drug Abuse from 1995 to 2002, "[Ecstasy] stimulates two types of activity. One, it causes a release of serotonin, and the other, it causes a release of dopamine, and the euphoria, the high, is actually a combination of these two chemical systems in the brain spiking."[15]

Serotonin and dopamine are both neurotransmitters, naturally occurring chemicals that are key in transmitting electrical impulses between the brain's neurons. Serotonin is believed to play a large part in regulating mood, sleep, and the brain's ability to recognize and react to pain. Ecstasy's first effect is to boost the brain's production of serotonin. When the brain is flooded with serotonin, the user begins to experience euphoria. At the same time ecstasy works to increase serotonin production, it also prevents the brain from storing or otherwise processing the excess, meaning that the brain stays flooded by serotonin until the drug wears off.

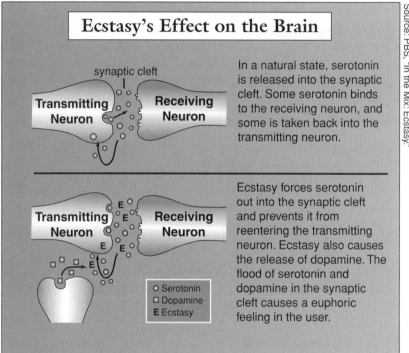

Ecstasy's Effect on the Brain

synaptic cleft

Transmitting Neuron

Receiving Neuron

In a natural state, serotonin is released into the synaptic cleft. Some serotonin binds to the receiving neuron, and some is taken back into the transmitting neuron.

Transmitting Neuron

Receiving Neuron

Ecstasy forces serotonin out into the synaptic cleft and prevents it from reentering the transmitting neuron. Ecstasy also causes the release of dopamine. The flood of serotonin and dopamine in the synaptic cleft causes a euphoric feeling in the user.

O Serotonin
□ Dopamine
E Ecstasy

Ecstasy also causes the brain to release dopamine, a neurotransmitter that has been linked to the experience of pleasure and the ability to control the body's movements. Researchers have long known that too little dopamine production shows itself in trembling and difficulty controlling the body's movements, as when people have Parkinson's disease. On the other hand, scientists believe that too much dopamine in certain regions of the brain causes the symptoms associated with schizophrenia. Research indicates that the release of dopamine is dependent on a previous release of serotonin. In general, then, ecstasy can be said to alter the balance of these two crucial neurotransmitters.

These changes in neurotransmitter levels and the sensations those changes produce eventually reverse themselves as the body gradually purges itself of ecstasy. Still, reports from people who have taken ecstasy suggest that there are longer-term consequences of ecstasy use.

Nightmares and Anxiety

One of the most commonly experienced aftereffects of ecstasy use is nightmares. Researchers are not certain of the chemical processes by which ecstasy causes the nightmares, but they believe it has something to do with the disturbance of serotonin levels, which play a large role in regulating sleep. One user recounted his experience with nightmares on the Web site ecstasy.org:

> Nightmares . . . always occur the night following the day that I have come down. . . . The dreams can be pretty frightening—3D full colour and sound experiences that sometimes end with my waking up, screaming, almost with my nails in the ceiling, scaring the hell out of my partner. . . . In such a post-E night I sometimes have ten to fifteen nightmares.[16]

Some ecstasy users experience frequent nightmares. Researchers believe that a disturbance in the brain's serotonin levels is the cause.

Besides nightmares, some users report anxiety—either stemming from worry over taking the drug or about decisions made while under the drug's influence. Other users report intense anxiety or panic attacks that seem to stem from physical effects of the drug. Some users report that even days or weeks after taking ecstasy they wake up in the night, experiencing intense fear, sweating, increased heart rate, and a tightening of the throat. Karl Jansen, a psychiatrist, says that this type of attack could have something to do with ecstasy's effect on neurotransmitter production, even though the levels of these chemicals in the brain have returned to normal: "The disturbance in serotonin creates a disturbance in the mechanism of sleep. . . . That the event occurs so long after taking the drugs does not discount this hypothesis. We are learning more about the long-term effects of drugs all the time."[17]

Jansen also believes that ecstasy blurs the boundary between consciousness and unconsciousness, opening the user up to the experience of nightmares: "The second explanation is psychological. Even just one E [ecstacy dose] will punch a hole in the wall between consciousness and unconsciousness, and lower defences against repressed psychic material. As you would expect, this material will start to come through in dreams."[18]

Anxiety

Ecstasy users have reported anxiety and panic attacks both during the rush period of the high and when coming down from the drug. Some long-term users experience such prolonged anxiety after using the drug that they are forced to turn to antianxiety medications like Paxil or Zoloft.

It is likely that the panic attacks experienced during the ecstasy high may be due to the intensity of the rush. Some psychologists hypothesize that the anxiety that can follow a night of ecstasy use may be social in nature; according to this theory, users may experience all of the insecurity and sensitivity that they were able to suppress during the ecstasy high. One user reported on the Web site erowid.org an experience with delayed social anxiety that led him to experience anxiety attacks:

Ecstasy users may experience anxiety, panic, and thoughts of suicide a few days after using the drug.

As I came down, I experienced huge uncertainty about the prudence of the decisions I made. . . . I feel very strongly that E caused me to form unnatural attachments to people, attachments that I feel weren't real, and to feel extremely hurt as these newfound relationships disintegrated. I read way too much into what was being said by me; I formed crushes that were exhausting to those I had them for.[19]

"Suicide Tuesdays"

Far more common than panic attacks is depression, which often sets in two or three days after ecstasy use. Since many who take ecstasy do so at parties held on weekends, the timing of the episodes of depression causes them to be called "terrible Tuesdays" or (more dramatically) "suicide Tuesdays." Some people experience severe headaches as well. Beck and Rosenbaum discuss the phenomenon in *Pursuit of Ecstasy:*

Heavy users in particular often saw the day(s) after as a time of survival, the discomfort justified only by the continued pleasures of the experience itself. Most respondents complained of mildly problematic aftereffects (fatigue, malaise, headaches) that often persisted for a day or two (and in rare cases longer) after taking MDMA.[20]

This depression appears to become more common and more severe the longer someone has been using ecstasy. Journalist Liz O'Brien describes her "suicide Tuesdays," noting that they become more frequent, longer, and ultimately more debilitating:

I noticed that the day after I'd taken ecstasy I felt blue and irritatingly lethargic. . . . As my use of the drug increased, so did the subsequent depression. Frequently, it lasted two or three days instead of one. I began to feel lost, and afraid. Also present was an undercurrent of insecurity: I constantly questioned myself.[21]

In their most extreme form, "suicide Tuesdays" can spur a user to take more ecstasy, setting in motion a cycle of dependence.

Physical Effects of Ecstasy

Researchers are continuing to learn more about the psychological effects of ecstasy use, coming to understand the chemical basis for these effects. Meanwhile, the physical effects of ecstasy are also

Initial Effects of Ecstasy

- Mental stimulation
- Emotional warmth
- Empathy
- Sense of well-being
- Decreased anxiety
- Enhanced sensory perception

- Nausea
- Chills
- Sweating
- Involuntary teeth clenching
- Muscle cramping
- Blurred vision

Source: National Institute on Drug Abuse, 2004.

better understood. For example, ecstasy stimulates release of large amounts of adrenaline, a hormone that raises blood pressure and heart rate. This combination is what allows those who take ecstasy at raves or clubs to dance for hours on end.

At the same time, while researchers do not know the chemical cause, ecstasy appears to suppress appetite and thirst. Many users also report that they experience dry mouth while high on ecstasy. Users may also experience skin irritation, blurred vision, chills, unsteadiness in walking, and insomnia in the days following their ecstasy high. Researchers are not certain what causes these and other effects such as chronic tics and movements, the most common of which is a grinding of the teeth. Many ecstasy users report that they grind their teeth so hard while high on ecstasy that they experience notable pain in their teeth and jaws the next day. Recent studies imply that frequent ecstasy use can lead to cracked enamel, worn teeth, and jaw problems. Hal Crossley, a dentist and associate professor of pharmacology at the University of Maryland Dental School, says, "I've seen users who have ground their teeth down to nubs. Their molars become flat, polished stumps. The back teeth go, and then the front teeth are just ground right down. The enamel in the front just dissolves away."[22]

Tolerance

Frequent users of ecstasy are at risk of becoming tolerant to the drug over time. In such individuals the drug loses some of its effectiveness, and the user must take greater amounts in order to attain the same high that was experienced in the beginning. Jansen describes a case in which a user injected 250 mg of MDMA powder intravenously up to four times a day for six months. Eventually, a dose of 250 mg taken orally had no effect at all. O'Brien describes her experience with the diminishing effects of the same dosage of ecstasy:

> I noticed I was no longer getting so high on the drug. While this phenomenon is common knowledge among users, the fact is downplayed in the media. The refrain "Are you feeling it?" . . . was replaced by "Are you feeling anything?" In order to feel the joy and abandon I had initially experienced, I had to down two tablets instead of one.[23]

Pacifiers as Rave Couture

At the height of raves' popularity during the 1990s, pacifiers were seen as a popular accessory to wear to the dance party. Many people believed that the pacifier was simply a fashion statement, but in fact, pacifiers are common accessories at raves and clubs where ecstasy is used. This is because chewing on a pacifier prevents teeth grinding, one of the most common side effects of ecstasy. "The first time I didn't use a pacifier, I definitely remembered it the next time. My jaw really hurt," claims Isabella, a seventeen-year-old user, in Mary Spicuzza's article "The Nightly Grind," which appeared on March 23, 2000 in the newspaper *Metro*. Many ravers grew accustomed to using pacifiers to alleviate jaw pain.

But dentists claim that pacifiers won't help protect an ecstasy user from long-term dental harm. "If someone uses pacifiers, it can cause orthodontic problems. If you hold it in the front and it pushes on the front teeth, it has the effect of thumb sucking," says dentist Steven Cohen in Spicuzza's article.

Because teeth grinding is a common side effect of ecstasy, pacifiers are common accessories at ecstasy raves.

Like O'Brien many users develop a pattern of taking larger and more frequent doses to attain the same high. Klam describes one such user in his *New York Times* article "Experiencing Ecstasy":

> [Kyle will] tell you it's not addictive—though he takes three pills in a night. For all those blissful weekends, he doesn't even seem happy. He's alternately euphoric and agitated. He might be better off seeing a counselor on campus to get that same sense of enlightenment. As for how MDMA has affected his brain, it's not clear. There might be no downside to taking it as much as he has—or he might be brain-damaged.[24]

In the extreme, tolerance can lead some to become "binge users," who take three to ten doses of ecstasy at a time and take repeated doses throughout their trip to lengthen it. Multiple doses, however, tend to increase the stimulant effects of ecstasy, but not the euphoria. Researcher Ronald Siegel observes, "When doses are pushed, we get madness, not ecstasy. I've seen people get ecstatic, and I've seen people crawl into fetal positions for three days."[25]

What is clear is that ecstasy has both pleasurable and negative effects. And it seems that the more we learn about ecstasy and its qualities, the more cause we have for concern.

Chapter 2

The Evolving Ecstasy Scene

Although ecstasy has been prescribed in the past for medical and therapeutic purposes, no formal studies have proven a significant benefit for patients. Ecstasy has come to be used exclusively as a recreational drug, taken for the high it produces. What alarms authorities is that since the mid-1970s, ecstasy has gone from a drug popular with urban professionals to a drug taken by teens attending raves and finally to a form of entertainment for a wide cross section of American youth.

Ecstasy Arrives on the Scene: The 1980s

In the early 1980s the same psychiatrists who had been experimenting with ecstasy as an aid to psychotherapy began to distribute MDMA as a recreational drug. The doctors had taken the drug themselves and found its effects pleasurable. At the time they also believed it was relatively harmless. Once these doctors supplied the drug to friends and acquaintances and these individuals experienced the high MDMA produced, demand increased quickly. Word of this newly discovered recreational drug spread across the nation. The psychiatrists, who became known as "the Boston group" because their practices were located in the Boston area, enlisted several regional distributors, but the scale of their operation was still too small to keep up with the demand for MDMA. Furthermore, the Boston group was still primarily interested in MDMA for therapeutic use and was not inclined to fulfill the recreational demand for the drug. They did, however, make one important contribution to the drug's street life: They gave MDMA the street name "ecstasy" in 1981. "Ecstasy was chosen for obvious reasons," recalls the unnamed dealer credited with creating the name, "because it would sell better than calling it Empathy. Empathy would be more appropriate, but how many people know what it means?"[26]

From Therapy to Recreation

Then in 1983 a Texas distributor for the Boston group concluded that since the recreational demand for ecstasy far exceeded his supply, he could make a lot of money by synthesizing and selling

In the 1980s ecstasy, still legal at the time, gained popularity as a recreational drug in big-city bars and clubs across the United States.

ecstasy on his own. As the Boston group was relatively uninterested in selling ecstasy as a recreational drug, he decided to form his own group of manufacturers and distributors to meet the demand. This organization became known as "the Texas group." Since ecstasy was not illegal, the Texas group was able to easily obtain the chemicals needed to make it. The Texas group began openly producing, marketing, and selling ecstasy. The Texans heavily marketed their product, throwing promotional "ecstasy parties" at bars and clubs in the Dallas and Austin areas. Eager to increase demand for their product, the Texas group aggressively marketed their product, putting up posters for their ecstasy parties that called the pills a "fun drug" that was "good to dance to."[27]

The Texas group's efforts were extremely successful. The drug's popularity surged, and the distributors teamed with bar owners to throw parties at which ecstasy was promoted. For their part, users viewed ecstasy as a fun, legal complement to alcohol. At this time the bulk of recreational use of ecstasy was still confined to Texas, although the drug was also a presence in large cities elsewhere in the country. Particularly attracted to ecstasy were young urban professionals (nicknamed "yuppies"), who considered the drug to be a stress reliever that did not interfere with their ability to hold a job. The drug became so popular with these busy young working people that the Texas media dubbed the drug "the yuppie psychedelic." These young adults claimed that ecstasy allowed them to indulge in "controlled hedonism"—meaning that they could let loose and enjoy themselves all night, but not have to worry about consequences like addiction or even the physical discomfort of hangovers.

The Texas of the early 1980s, flush with oil money and young, well-off professionals, proved to be the perfect place to launch a fun and seemingly harmless drug like ecstasy. In their book *The Book of E: All About Ecstasy*, Push and Mireille Silcott describe the money-charged atmosphere:

> In 1984, the oil boom that had begun in the mid-Seventies had caught up with Texan society. New people were wealthy, not just from oil, but from anything. . . . *Dallas*, the TV show, was not too far off the mark in its se-

quined day suits and gaggle of chauffeurs. Texas did feel that way—almost as if you could swipe the air in front of you and cash would flow out of the nothingness, like the atmosphere itself jangled with coins and promise. The time was ripe, maybe over-ripe, for something like the Starck club [known for its huge parties where ecstasy was used] to open up.[28]

Celebrities and wealthy locals attended this Dallas nightspot, and ecstasy attained incredible popularity there, since the drug was legal and also considered a status symbol. The Silcotts describe the Starck club:

> It was hard to get to the bars to buy the Starck's 100 per cent pure XTC pills. The crowds waving money at the barmaids were always four deep. There were free-floating dealers from whom it was usually easier to procure the drug. Some of the dealers wore t-shirts emblazoned with X, or even ones proclaiming Buy My XTC. [DJ Kerry] Jaggers estimates that 70 per cent of those visiting Starck did buy it. "Without any guilt or any stigma," [he says]. "It was not seen as other drugs were. It was seen as high class."[29]

Aside from its general popularity among urban professionals in Texas, ecstasy found devotees in the gay communities of big cities elsewhere. For example, it was popular at the Saint, a gay disco in New York City, where many patrons liked ecstasy's empathetic effects and loosening of inhibitions. DJ Kerry Jaggers was also a frequent patron of the Saint, and he remembers how the drug seemed to help users accept their sexuality:

> Everyone else I knew [used ecstasy.] But the drug was never the focus, the drug—legal, remember—was no more controversial than baby powder. . . . Ecstasy is something that takes down your inhibition. . . . Nobody thought about it, or talked about it, but as the drug became more and more popular, I watched it change the Saint. Change from a buncha guys who were . . . *scared* of their sexuality. *Scared* of being found out. *Scared* of each other. These people blossomed and bloomed. I had never seen anything like it.[30]

Ecstasy may have been seen as relatively harmless at this point, but the drug was beginning to gain the attention of government officials, in part because of who was using it. Not only were yuppies using the drug at expensive nightclubs, but the drug was becoming popular among students at Southern

In the mid-1980s Texas senator Lloyd Bentsen condemned ecstasy use among college students. The drug became illegal soon afterward.

Methodist University in Dallas, a prestigious institution attended by the sons and daughters of well-known politicians. Nightclubber Wade Hampton recalls:

> The SMU students usually weren't connected to the club scene, so for them, ecstasy wasn't something with which to complement a fun night, it was a context-less thing to get [messed] up with, beer-bash stuff. . . . They were *politicians'* kids. Their parents were all friends with [then Vice President] George Bush, for God's sake. They were the death knell for legal ecstasy, those kids.[31]

One politician who took particular notice was Texas Senator Lloyd Bentsen, a Democrat who sat on the Senate Judiciary Committee. Bentsen was disturbed by reports of the drug's growing use, considering that so little was known about its long-term effects. He spoke out in favor of banning ecstasy.

After Bentsen drew attention to the drug, the Texas media also began to raise questions about ecstasy's widespread use and possible dangers. Responding to the ecstasy controversy, the *Dallas Morning News* reported on March 3, 1985, "The drug problem is not something that went away after the psychedelic Sixties, or something happening in other cities in bad areas to bad families. It's here."[32] Local papers characterized ecstasy as a seedy street drug, a "superamphetamine" that could ruin lives. Texas journalists wrote editorials in which they worried that ecstasy might become an epidemic, blighting inner cities and bringing drug-related violence, as crack cocaine was doing at the time.

As it became clear that the government might well ban ecstasy, the prospect caused the Texas group, still the drug's largest manufacturer and distributor, to step up production to cash in on what appeared to be the drug's limited days of legality. It is estimated that they went from producing roughly one thousand tablets a day to eight thousand a day. In the few months before MDMA was criminalized, the Texas group produced an estimated 2 million ecstasy tablets.

How Ecstasy Became Illegal

As concerns grew about ecstasy and the explosive growth in its use, the Food and Drug Administration (FDA), the federal agency that studies all drugs to determine which ones may be dangerous to users, took action. Usually, if the FDA suspects that a drug poses a threat to the public, it notifies the DEA, which assigns it to one of five categories known as schedules. The schedule a drug is assigned to depends on the DEA's perception of the danger it poses—for example, its addictive potential or dangerous side effects. Drugs determined to pose lesser dangers and to have some

The Controlled Substances Act

According to Julie Holland, editor of *Ecstasy: The Complete Guide,* here are the definitions of the various schedules as laid out by the Controlled Substances Act.

Schedule I

A. The drug or other substance has a high potential for abuse.

B. The drug or other substance has no currently accepted medical use in treatment in the United States.

C. There is a lack of accepted safety for use of the drug or other substance under medical supervision.

Schedule II

A. The drug or other substance has a high potential for abuse.

B. The drug or other substance has a currently accepted medical use in treatment in the United States or a currently accepted medical use with severe restrictions.

C. Abuse of the drug or other substances may lead to severe psychological or physical dependence.

Schedule III

A. The drug or other substance has a potential for abuse less than the drugs or other substances on Schedules I and II.

B. The drug or other substance has a currently accepted medical use in treatment in the United States.

C. Abuse of the drug or other substance may lead to moderate or minimal physical dependence or high psychological dependence.

Schedule IV

A. The drug or other substance has a low potential for abuse relative to the drugs or other substances on Schedule III.

B. The drug or other substance has a currently accepted medical use in the United States.

C. Abuse of the drug or other substance may lead to limited physical dependence or psychological dependence relative to the drugs or other substances in Schedule III.

Schedule V

A. The drug or other substance has a low potential for abuse relative to the drugs or other substances in Schedule IV.

B. The drug or other substance has a currently accepted medical use in the United States.

C. Abuse of the drug or other substance may lead to limited physical dependence or psychological dependence relative to the drugs or other substances in Schedule IV.

medical value—what the public would consider "prescription drugs"—are legally available within limits as Schedule III, IV, and V drugs. Drugs determined to pose greater dangers to users, such as morphine and cocaine, are Schedule II drugs and are strictly controlled and may only be prescribed for specific medical purposes. A Schedule I drug is believed to have no medical value and cannot be prescribed by physicians or even tested in controlled experiments. This category includes heroin and LSD.

In response to Bentsen's concerns, the DEA scheduled hearings at which doctors, scientists, and law enforcement officials were invited to express their opinions on just how restricted ecstasy should be. In the meantime, Bentsen had in 1984 already convinced the DEA that ecstasy should be "emergency scheduled," meaning that it was made illegal even before the hearings

In 1988 DEA director John C. Lawn classified ecstasy as a Schedule I illegal drug with no approved medical uses.

took place. This rare emergency scheduling is reserved for drugs thought to be very dangerous. In communicating with the DEA, Bentsen presented two facts that he felt implied ecstasy's danger to the public: that MDA, a drug chemically similar to ecstasy, had been proven to cause brain damage in rats. Also, while ecstasy was most popular in Texas, there was evidence of recreational use taking place in twenty-eight states, meaning that its use was spreading.

After ecstasy was emergency scheduled, the hearings to discuss the drug's dangers and potential benefits took place in February, June, and July of 1985. A number of psychotherapists claiming that ecstasy had beneficial effects on their patients attended the hearings. But they had no scientific documentation of ecstasy's benefits; no controlled studies had been done, and thus it was impossible to prove that ecstasy had been responsible for breakthroughs they recounted. Judge Francis Young, who presided over the hearings, recommended that ecstasy be made illegal for all but clinical use and research. This classification, by stopping short of an outright ban, would have allowed physicians to prescribe the drug to patients.

John C. Lawn, the DEA administrator at the time, used his authority and ignored Judge Young's recommendation. He felt that because the drug had not been approved by the FDA, and because it had no medically proven benefit, it should be illegal in all circumstances. Ecstasy was formally listed as a Schedule I, illegal drug with no medical use on March 23, 1988.

With the DEA's ruling, psychotherapists had no choice but to stop prescribing ecstasy for their patients. Advocates of ecstasy's use in therapy were stunned, because they believed that the drug posed no threat to their patients, who used the drug in a completely different setting than recreational users. "It was as if I had discovered how to use oil paints in my art," recalls psychiatrist George Greer, "and then all the paints were banned because people were sniffing them."[33]

Patients who had benefited from MDMA-assisted therapy were also shocked by the drug's illegal status. Many patients credited

Herbal Ecstasy

When ecstasy was made illegal in 1985, some stores began marketing a substance that they called "herbal ecstasy." Also known as Rave Energy, Cloud 9, X, or Ultimate Xphoria, herbal ecstasy is a compound that its sellers claim produces many of the same effects as ecstasy. Mostly ephedrine and caffeine, the compound stimulates the cardiovascular and nervous system. While legal, herbal ecstasy is not actually that much safer than ecstasy. Ephedrine is often sold in health stores, and is used in the United States to spur weight loss, boost energy, and enhance athletic performance. But ephedrine is considered dangerous by many health professionals. Since 1994 the FDA has received seventeen reports of ephedrine-related deaths, and more than eight hundred reports of negative reactions to ephedrine, including hypertension (elevated blood pressure), palpitations (rapid heart rate), neuropathy (nerve damage), myopathy (muscle injury), psychosis, stroke, memory loss, heart rate irregularities, insomnia, nervousness, tremors, seizures, and heart attacks. The FDA is seeking to prohibit the marketing of dietary supplements containing 8 milligrams or more of ephedrine alkaloids per serving, but their ability to control the sale of ephedrine is limited, because the herb is categorized as a "dietary supplement" and not a drug.

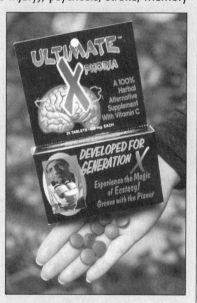

Once ecstasy was banned, herbal ecstasy products became available in large numbers.

MDMA for the success of their treatment, and had difficulty accepting that a powerful tool was being taken away from their therapists. "I cannot believe that this isn't available to people in the way that I was benefited,"[34] says Kathy Tamm, a patient who was treated with MDMA in 1983.

Ecstasy as a "Rave Drug": the 1990s

Even before the DEA's formal move to ban ecstasy, the profile of the typical user was changing. The Starck club was raided in September 1986, leading to the arrest of thirty-six people and the seizure of $10,000 worth of drugs, mostly ecstasy and cocaine. The Texans who had been manufacturing ecstasy stopped production, meaning that ecstasy was not only illegal but in shorter supply. Demand, however, continued, although not from young urban professionals but from younger users. In the late 1980s a new type of dance party was gaining popularity. These gatherings, called "raves," began appearing in San Francisco. Raves were essentially large parties staged in abandoned warehouses or outdoors in parks or other open spaces. Technohouse music was played, and many who attended were attracted to what they claimed was a loving, accepting ambience. "The first parties I went to were kind of life-changing events," says Legba, a twenty-one-

By the early 1990s ecstasy had become the drug of choice for ravers who wished to dance all night without stopping to rest.

year-old college student from Virginia, "because people were to-tally accepting of everybody, however they looked or danced, and that completely blew me away."[35]

Rave promoters generally discouraged alcohol use, but ecstasy was another matter. Despite their illegality, ecstasy pills were sold openly; for many people the rave experience was unimaginable without taking ecstasy. The burst of energy that ecstasy users experience, along with the suppression of appetite and thirst, made it possible for ravers to dance all night without taking a break. The hallucinogenic effects made the music, strobe lights, and other visual effects such as glow sticks and wild decorations seem hypnotic. In his book *Generation Ecstasy*, Simon Reynolds recalls the sensation of taking ecstasy at a rave:

> The blitz of noise and lights at a rave tilts the MDMA experience toward the drug's purely sensuous and sensational effects. . . . All music sounds better on E—crisper and more distinct, but also engulfing in its immediacy. . . . You feel like you're dancing inside the music; sound becomes a fluid medium in which you're immersed.[36]

In 1992 raves spread from San Francisco to Los Angeles and soon began showing up all over California. The phenomenon soon spread to the East Coast as well. In December of that year, Frankie Bones, a New York native who had been performing as a DJ in England, decided to hold a rave on an abandoned loading dock in Queens, New York. Over five thousand kids from New York and neighboring states attended. The rave was such a success that attendees began holding raves of their own in their home states. Throughout 1993 and 1994 the rave phenomenon spread across America, and raves soon appeared in every state. As more and more teens attended raves, the number who experimented with ecstasy also grew phenomenally.

As more young people became familiar with ecstasy's music- and dance-enhancing effects, the demand for ecstasy entered another arena: the dance club. Although the dance club atmosphere is similar to the rave atmosphere, the clubs were generally operated legally. That meant that ecstasy generally was not openly sold or used. Still, plenty of dance club patrons used the drug. Now ecstasy was everywhere: in the urban areas where dance clubs are common, and in the rural areas where raves were often put on.

Today it is extremely difficult to make generalizations about ecstasy users, because as the drug has become more widely known, its use has invaded almost every pocket of society. Ecstasy appears to be a drug that can perform many different functions, and as time goes on and the drug's popularity grows, many users seem to agree with Alexander Shulgin's contention that ecstasy "could be all things to all people."[37] Journalist Jessica Reaves writes in *Time* magazine, "While still popular with black-clad, street-smart city kids . . . ecstasy has now begun to infiltrate the suburbs as well as college frat houses and dorm parties from Oregon to Virginia."[38]

Easier to Get—and Easier to Use

Even though ecstasy is illegal, it is not particularly expensive. Whereas prices for ecstasy once averaged $25 per pill, competition among dealers has reportedly driven prices down so that the drug sells for as little as $8 per pill. These lower prices have increased the drug's popularity in low-income areas. Furthermore, as the drug has spread beyond wealthy white suburbs, it has transcended ethnic lines and is now equally popular in African American and Hispanic neighborhoods. In a 2000 survey conducted by *Pulse Check*, a White House publication, 56 percent of law enforcement officials claimed that ecstasy was "widely available" in their area; an additional 35 percent described the drug as "somewhat available."[39]

The easy access to ecstasy meant that people began to use it not just to help them "let loose" or dance all night. Now it has become part of some youths' everyday existence. Journalist John Cloud recounted the following scenario in a June 2000 *Time* magazine article:

> Cobb County, GA, May 11, 2000. It's a Thursday morning, and 18-year-old "Karen" and five friends decide to go for it. They skip first period and sneak into the woods near their upscale high school. One of them takes

The low cost of ecstasy in recent years has made the drug extremely popular among diverse segments of American society.

out six rolls—six ecstasy pills—and they each swallow one. Then back to school, flying on a drug they once used only on weekends. Now they smile stupid gelatinous smiles at one another, even as high school passes them by. That night they will go out and drop more ecstasy, rolling into the early hours of another school day.[40]

It is clear that more and more Americans are using ecstasy for recreation. With ecstasy's popularity on the rise and its long-term effects unclear, government and law enforcement officials have made containing the spread of ecstasy a high priority.

Chapter 3

The Dangers of Ecstasy

With ecstasy use rising so rapidly across many different sectors of American society, more and more people are becoming concerned about the consequences of using this drug. Certainly, it appears that teens' awareness of the dangers of ecstasy is on the rise. In 2002, 45.7 percent of twelveth-graders surveyed felt that there was a "great risk" in trying ecstasy, compared with 37.9 percent in 2001. Yet authorities remain concerned by the numbers of Americans who still see MDMA as being relatively harmless, when in fact, some studies indicate that it may be a neurotoxin—a chemical that causes permanent damage to the brain. "These are not just benign, fun drugs," says Alan Leshner, the director of the National Institute on Drug Abuse. "They carry serious short-term and long-term dangers."[41]

Impure or Fake Ecstasy Pills

One danger of ecstasy use stems from its status as an illegal drug. For drugs sold legally in the United States, the FDA requires that manufacturers test samples to ensure that the products contain no impurities and that the doses are consistent for all batches. However, nobody runs such tests on illegal drugs. In the case of ecstacy, the pills are almost never pure. The MDMA is most commonly mixed with caffeine, ephedrine, or amphetamines. All of these "mixers" have effects of their own that are added to those of MDMA. Such additional drugs may further raise heart rate and body temperature, for example, increasing the risk of heart failure or heatstroke.

Sometimes, pills sold as ecstasy may actually contain another drug entirely. One common substitute for ecstasy is a cough suppressant called dextromethorphan (DXM), the active ingredient

Authorities remain deeply concerned over the number of Americans who view ecstasy as a harmless drug that carries no long-term risks.

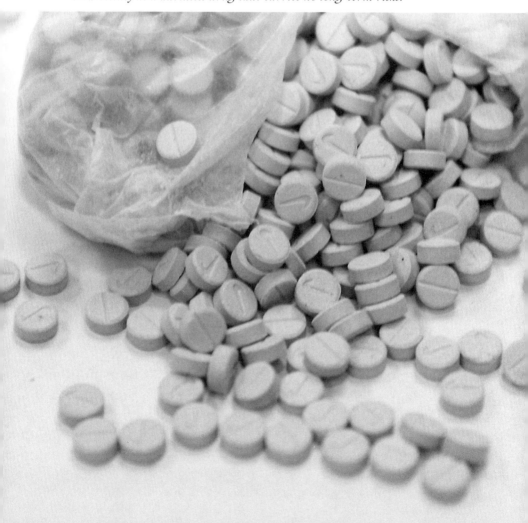

found in many over-the-counter cough medicines. While DXM is
not especially dangerous on its own, if someone later takes a pill
that really does contain ecstasy, the combination amplifies both
drugs' overheating effects, possibly leading to heatstroke.

An even more dangerous substitute for ecstasy is a drug called
paramethoxyamphetamine (PMA), sold on the street under the
name "white Mitsubishi." Its effects are similar to, but weaker
than, those of ecstasy. According to the White House Office of
Drug Policy:

> PMA (paramethoxyamphetamine) is an illicit, synthetic hallucinogen that
> has stimulant effects similar to MDMA. However, when users take PMA
> thinking they are really ingesting MDMA, they often think they have taken
> weak ecstasy because PMA's effects take longer to appear. They then in-
> gest more of the substance to attain a better high, which can result in over-
> dose death.[42]

As the problems of mixing ecstasy with DXM or PMA illustrate,
mixing ecstasy with other substances can be dangerous. The result
of mixing ecstasy with substances like alcohol, amphetamines, or
antidepressants can be side effects that are deadly.

Hyperthermia

Even taken alone, ecstasy occasionally has extremely dangerous
side effects. The most common of these is hyperthermia, or overheating. This is a serious, even deadly, condition that occurs because ecstasy tends to suppress the user's normal instinct to slow
down when the body's temperature rises to levels that cannot be
protected by sweating.

Symptoms of hyperthermia include dilated pupils, sweating
(though sweating often ceases in the most severe cases), an increased heart rate (often in the range of 140 to 160 beats per
minute), low blood pressure, and seizures. The body's core temperature rises to between 102.2 and 107.6 degrees Fahrenheit
(39° to 42°C), although ecstasy users have been known to show
up in emergency rooms with core temperatures as high as 109 degrees Fahrenheit (42.8°C). Temperatures this high commonly
lead to liver failure and/or kidney failure, swelling of the brain,

and a breakdown of muscle tissue known as rhabdomyolysis. This latter condition can cause high potassium levels, which lead to fatal irregularities in heart rhythms.

The circumstances under which most people use ecstasy, in hot, crowded nightclubs, make hyperthermia even more likely. John A. Henry, a clinical psychologist specializing in drug and alcohol abuse, has said that the risk from hyperthermia resulting from taking ecstacy may be "due mainly to the circumstances in which it is misused."[43] For example, writer Matthew Klam describes the extremely crowded conditions at a 2000 rave that could contribute to hyperthermia:

> After everything I'd read, all the mountains of warnings against hyperthermia, I was shocked when I got to the jungle room [where the dancing took place] and the temperature was, easily, nine hundred million degrees. Kids were lying on the floor, either because they'd died or fainted or because they hoped it might be cooler down there. The entire club was now a Tokyo subway car packed at rush hour. You had to put your arms over your head to squeeze through. In a matter of two hours, this place had become really uncomfortable.[44]

In rare cases, hyperthermia is suspected of playing a role in fatal heart attacks. In the *Washington Monthly*, Benjamin Wallace-Wells comments on this factor:

> In a few, extremely rare cases, and particularly when users have been dancing vigorously—a hallmark of the rave culture—ecstasy seems to be linked to sudden heart attacks in healthy young people who do not appear otherwise disposed to heart failure. . . . Researchers have speculated that it [ecstasy] somehow suppresses the body's ability to sense dramatic increases in its own temperature, leading the heart to over-pump and overheat the body; some also suspect that the deaths might be largely due to impure ecstasy cut with amphetamines, which are known to increase users' heart rates.[45]

Hyperthermia is treatable, but must be dealt with quickly. Doctors give the victim intravenous saline solution, which helps reverse dehydration. In cases where the patient is having seizures, doctors administer a sedative such as Valium. In more severe cases, ice baths may be required to bring down the victim's temperature.

Taking ecstasy in hot, crowded nightclubs makes users extremely susceptible to hyperthermia, or overheating.

Hyponatremia

Sometimes, possibly in an attempt to stave off hyperthermia, an ecstasy user will drink an excessive amount of water. In a few cases, the victim takes in so much water that the sodium concentration in the blood drops to dangerously low levels. Making this condition more likely is ecstasy's tendency to increase the secretion of a hormone called vasopressin (antidiuretic hormone, or ADH), which causes the kidneys to reabsorb water rather than excrete it.

Hyponatremia can be fatal. In extreme cases, the brain swells, a condition known as cerebral edema. In 1995 Leah Betts died in the United Kingdom on her eighteenth birthday after taking only one dose of ecstasy. Exactly how much water Leah drank is in dispute; news reports said that Leah had drunk over a gallon of water at one time. In an interview, her mother recalled being summoned to the bathroom after hearing that Leah was in trouble: "She was in the bathroom with her back to me, leaning over the washbasin. When she turned around, her eyes were black, like eyes in a horror film. Her pupils were dilated and there were no irises. I asked her what she'd been up to and she told me she'd taken an ecstasy tablet."[46] The swelling of the brain that can result from hyponatremia is sometimes so extreme that the brain is forced into the top of the spine, a condition known as "coning," since the opening of the spinal column is cone-shaped.

Serotonin syndrome

Another potential danger of ecstasy use, although rarer than hyperthermia and hyponatremia, is serotonin syndrome. Ecstasy causes the brain to produce a flood of serotonin, which is responsible for the euphoria that users experience. Sometimes, however, this excess of serotonin overwhelms the parts of the brain that control the heart and regulate blood pressure. In 10 to 15 percent of cases, serotonin syndrome is fatal.

Although this extreme overload of serotonin is rare, there is no predicting who will experience it, since the problem can occur in someone who has taken a single dose of ecstasy. Furthermore, when serotonin syndrome occurs, death can follow within minutes. It is imperative, then, that if symptoms such as confusion, difficulty waking, or involuntary muscle spasms (among others) are observed, the victim must be rushed to a hospital.

Controversy over Long-Term Dangers

Conditions such as hyperthermia, hyponatremia, and serotonin syndrome all become apparent relatively quickly after ecstasy is taken. What worries scientists and policy makers even more are ecstasy's long-term effects, which are largely unknown or in dispute. A few studies have been done using animals, and a few studies have been conducted on humans who have admitted using ecstasy and other drugs. In both cases, questions over methodology or the researcher's scientific integrity make it difficult to evaluate the results.

Much of the most controversial research has been done by George A. Ricaurte of Johns Hopkins University. Data from many of Ricaurte's studies imply that ecstasy is a neurotoxin, meaning that it causes permanent damage to the brain. However, many of his fellow scientists have questioned whether Ricaurte's methods can be trusted. He has been accused, for example, of allowing human test subjects to be tested when they were sleep-deprived or high on other drugs. Donald G. McNeil Jr. describes one such research subject, Greg M., in the *New York Times:*

> Although the two [Greg and a friend] used many drugs, the research assistant who interviewed them by phone told them what not to admit to her if they wanted to be in the study. . . . They and other ecstasy users flown in from the West Coast took memory tests while still jet-lagged, they said. Then after lumbar punctures to check serotonin levels, neither

Dangers of Ecstasy

Short Term	Long Term
• Hyperthermia (overheating)	• Possible damage to serotonin system, leading to:

• Serotonin syndrome (potentially fatal excess of serotonin)	– sleep disturbances
	  – mood disorders
	  – decreased memory

• Hyponatremia (dangerously low sodium levels in the blood)	• Psychological addiction

Source: Holland, *Ecstasy: The Complete Guide.*

The Controversial Research of George Ricaurte

One study that Ricaurte published on ecstasy in 2002, which found that even one average dose could cause extensive brain damage or death in animals, was eventually discredited when it was discovered that the test subjects in the study, a group of monkeys, had actually been given a much more potent methamphetamine commonly known as speed, not ecstasy. Two of the ten monkeys in the study died, and two others collapsed of heatstroke. Fellow scientists questioned the study right away, in light of the fact that of the people who have tried it (estimated at around 10 million people in the United States) only a few have died. Ricaurte claimed that the substitution was an accident, but fellow scientists accused him of trying to manipulate his results to cater to officials in the National Institute on Drug Abuse, which was looking for concrete data that would allow the government to increase penalties for ecstasy sale and use. In 2003 Ricaurte in the journal *Science* retracted the study and explained the mistake. The British journal *Nature*, quoted in Carla Spartos's article "The Ecstasy Factor," which appeared in the *Village Voice* on March 10, 2004, called the incident "one of the more bizarre episodes in the history of drug research." On the ABC News special "Ecstasy Rising," Peter Jennings likened the government's embrace of Ricaurte's doomsaying research to the familiar parable of the boy who cried wolf. "The U.S. government's claim that ecstasy causes devastating, irreversible brain damage was a dramatic exaggeration of the risk. . . . The risk of death is minuscule, overstating this risk is not going to stop [users] from taking the drug." Ricaurte insisted in Spartos's article, "Everyone in the field has accepted [that MDMA] is a neurotoxin. I think those [dissenting] arguments have to be put in perspective."

was given the usual night's rest to prevent fierce headaches. They had to carry their backpacks across campus and be wired up for a sleep study, which Greg argued could not reflect normal sleep patterns because they were in pain.[47]

Ricaurte has admitted to including sleep-deprived or jet-lagged subjects in his studies, but points out that such irregularities were always noted in his papers. He asserts that his staff quizzed volunteers to weed out those using other drugs, and performed blood and urine tests to verify subjects' answers (though he has admitted that hair tests would have been more accurate).

More controversial were study results Ricaurte published in 2002 that concluded, based on experiments on rhesus monkeys, that ecstasy produces severe and potentially lethal damage to the brain. Ricaurte's results were discredited when it was discovered that the monkeys were given not ecstasy but a much more potent substance, methamphetamine. Ricaurte claimed that the substitution was an accident, but many of his fellow scientists questioned how such a fundamental mistake could take place in a respected laboratory.

Ecstasy expert Julie Holland told McNeil, "It's hard to trust George." She has accused him of "playing games with his data"[48] to win more federal grants; he has already been awarded more than $10 million from the National Institute on Drug Abuse (NIDA). Richard J. Wurtman, a clinician at Harvard and M.I.T., concurs, accusing Ricuarte in McNeil's *New York Times* article of "running a cottage industry showing that everything under the sun is neurotoxic."[49]

Is Ecstasy a Neurotoxin?

It is generally accepted that using ecstasy causes the brain to flood with serotonin, and that serotonin levels then dip below normal in the days following use and stay that way for some time. As Simon Reynolds explains in his book *Generation Ecstasy*, "Taking ecstasy is like going on an emotional spree, spending your happiness in advance. With irregular use, such extravagance isn't a problem. But with sustained and excessive use, the brain's serotonin levels can become seriously depleted, so that it takes around six weeks of abstinence from MDMA to restore normal levels."[50]

Several studies Ricaurte has done on animals—most commonly rhesus monkeys—imply that the serotonin levels of frequent ecstasy users may never return to normal levels. Ricaurte has concluded that frequent ecstasy use can permanently damage the serotonin system in the brain. The White House Office of Drug Policy concludes from this research that "MDMA damages neurons that use serotonin to communicate with other neurons in the brain."[51] Furthermore, since serotonin plays a role in controlling sleep and mood, some experts worry that those who use ecstasy frequently may experience lifelong sleep disturbances, mood disorders, or memory problems. For instance, some users say that they are irritable and depressed long after the drug's other effects have worn off. Kati Stephenson, a Florida teen who by her own admission is psychologically addicted to ecstasy, told CBS News, "I don't get happy like normal people anymore. So I have to take antidepressants for that."[52] Damage to the serotonin system could explain the tendency of some users to become dependent on the drug, even though it is not physically addictive.

Frequent use of ecstasy may permanently damage the brain's serotonin system, putting habitual users at risk for serious depression.

Psychological Addiction

Some users take more ecstasy to relieve the depression they feel when the drug starts to wear off. Still, ecstasy is not physically addictive, meaning that a user's cells do not become dependent on the presence of the drug to function properly. The behavior of animals allowed to self-administer hits of ecstasy implies that while animals will make some effort to get the drug, they will not put themselves in harm's way to obtain another dose. This is different from the response to physically addictive drugs like heroin. Furthermore, once the user stops using ecstasy, he or she will not experience painful, long-lasting physical withdrawal symptoms, such as muscle spasms and nausea.

Although the drug is not physically addictive, the organization DanceSafe.org, whose members try to reduce drug abuse among club goers, points out, "The drug can often take on great importance in people's lives, and some people become rather compul-

A serotonin molecule is depicted in this computer model. Using ecstasy causes the brain to flood with the neurotransmitter.

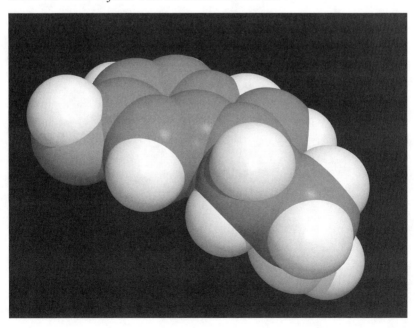

sive in their use."[53] NIDA's former director, Alan Leshner, agrees that ecstasy is still psychologically addictive:

> There's no such thing as recreational ecstasy use; this is not like playing ping-pong or tennis. We are very concerned because of its rise in popularity or how people claim that it doesn't have a big effect. . . . Whether or not it produces physical dependence is not relevant. Methamphetamine and crack cocaine don't cause physical dependence according to physical medical criteria, but they are among the most addicting substances ever known to mankind.[54]

Rehabilitation centers have recently begun to report an increase in the number of people seeking treatment for psychological addiction to ecstasy. While their bodies may not be dependent on MDMA, many users come to believe that they cannot feel happy without the drug. This vicious cycle is what Kati Stephenson, an active and popular high school student, became caught up in: "I would go home and, if I didn't have any more drugs, I would be so depressed and just lay in bed for two or three days. I would just have no motivation to do anything."[55]

Supporting Evidence

While studies suggesting that ecstasy use has long-term negative consequences remain controversial, at least one autopsy on a human ecstasy user seems to support the idea that the serotonin system may be permanently damaged by this drug. In 2000 four scientists studied brain tissue from a deceased heavy MDMA user, and found that serotonin levels in a part of the brain known as the striatum were significantly lower than normal.

Una McCann, an associate professor in the Department of Psychiatrics at Johns Hopkins University who is married to George Ricaurte, adds that the damage ecstasy causes may be subtle and only become apparent much later:

> Most people who use MDMA don't die or have psychiatric problems right afterward. This makes people think it's safe. I think the danger is people are slowly damaging their brains and are totally unaware of it. I think the older they get, the [users] will be much more vulnerable to a variety of problems such as depression, memory disturbances, anxiety disorders and sleep difficulties.[56]

On the other hand, some scientists believe that ecstasy does not damage the serotonin system. James P. O'Callaghan, head of the molecular neurotoxicology lab at the federal government's Centers for Disease Control and Prevention, doubts that ecstasy is highly neurotoxic. He argues that the fact that the drug has an effect is evidence the serotonin mechanism is unharmed: "From a scientific standpoint, there is no evidence that it causes brain damage in humans. Because these drugs act by releasing serotonin, you have to have terminals there for the drug to act on. By definition, you can't be destroying the machinery if the drug continues to work."[57]

What some research indicates is that if ecstasy does damage the brain's neurotransmitter production, that harm might not be permanent. According to Mark Laurelle of the New York State Psychiatric Institute, "In people who had used ecstasy, but who had stopped taking ecstasy for two or three months, normal serotonin function was found. There was indeed a reduced serotonin function but that reduction may be reversible after 2–3 months of abstinence."[58]

Part of the difficulty of determining whether there is a link between ecstasy and brain damage is that the potency of the drug as it is taken in a recreational setting is variable and hard to measure. One study of the effects of low doses of ecstasy on rhesus monkeys conducted by Ricaurte found little if any sign of damage to the brain's serotonin or dopamine systems. Still, these animals were receiving carefully managed doses of ecstasy in a laboratory—not pills of uncertain composition and potency.

Memory Impairment

Researcher Gerald Valentine concedes that the research on the harm ecstasy does is not conclusive: "To date, a clearly defined psychiatric or neurological syndrome has not been attributed to ecstasy abuse."[59] Still, some experts remain concerned. "The serotonin system, which is compromised by MDMA, is fundamental to the brain's integration of information and emotion," says Leshner. "At the very least, people who take MDMA, even just a few

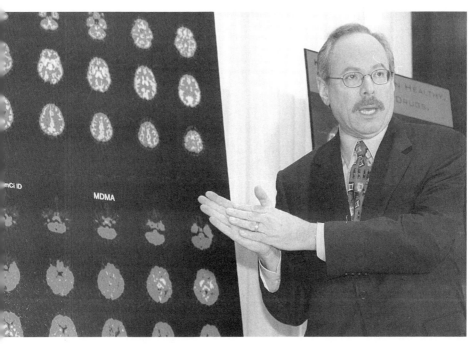

During a 2000 press conference, Alan Leshner, director of the National Institute on Drug Abuse, uses MRI images to illustrate the harmful effects of ecstasy on the brain.

times, are risking long-term, perhaps permanent, problems with learning and memory."[60]

Decreased Memory

One reason experts worry about the potential for harm to memory is that ecstasy is known to affect the hippocampus, the part of the brain involved in learning and storing of new information. The potential for memory impairment seems clearest among those who use ecstasy more than twice a month. The results of a study at the University of Toronto, published in 2001 in the journal *Neurology*, indicated that ecstasy seemed to harm the memory of human subjects. This study was based on the performance on tests by fifteen ecstasy users, ages seventeen to thirty-one, over a year-long period. The subjects reported taking ecstasy an average of

2.4 times per month. The researchers put participants through a variety of tests, including one in which subjects read short passages and were asked to recall them either right away or after a brief pause. The *New York Times* reported some of the results: "Over the course of the year . . . the ecstasy users' ability to recall the passages after a delay declined by about half."[61]

Two previous British studies, one by Michael J. Morgan of the University of Swansea in 1999 and one by Jacqui Rodgers of Newcastle University in 2000, also indicated that exposure to ecstasy does appear to cause memory impairment. The Morgan study looked into the possible medium and long-term memory effects of ecstasy. It also sought to differentiate the effects of ecstasy from the effects of using other drugs. There were three groups of test subjects: twenty-five MDMA users, twenty-two users of multiple drugs other than ecstasy, and nineteen "non–drug user" control subjects (though some of these controls did use alcohol or cigarettes). Each group had similar levels of education. All of the ecstasy users had used MDMA on at least twenty occasions. Researchers administered story recall tests to all three groups to test both immediate and delayed memory. The MDMA users performed worse on the memory tests than both the control group and the group using multiple drugs.

The Rodgers study also tested three groups of subjects: fifteen regular users of ecstasy, fifteen regular users of marijuana who had never taken ecstasy, and fifteen subjects who had never taken any kind of illegal drug. The researchers administered a memory test and a computerized reaction time test on a day when the subjects claimed not to have taken any drugs. The subjects were also asked to complete a biographical questionnaire and the Cognitive Failures Questionnaire (CFQ) in order to assess the subjects' own admitted memory failures. All three groups exhibited similar reaction time to various stimuli. They also all had similar ability to remember images they had seen and had similar attention and concentration abilities. But the researchers found significant impairment in verbal memory—that is, memory of things they heard—in both the marijuana and ecstasy users. The researchers also found a significant impairment among ecstasy users in performance of tasks that required recalling information after a brief delay. Despite these findings, all of the groups self-reported similar memory failures, meaning that neither the marijuana nor the ecstasy users were aware of their own memory impairments.

Another British study at the University of Northumbria supports the idea that heavy ecstasy use can impair memory. Tracking the performance of a group of clubgoers who took ecstasy between eight and ten times a month, the researchers found that "they had significant memory problems: they would forget such things as setting their alarm clocks, and they had difficulty with long-term episodic memory, forgetting to pass on messages."[62] The users also had problems with "queued memory," often referred to as "working memory," or the memory that allows one to remember basic tasks and complete them.

Tom Heffernan, one of the Northumbria study's authors, also expressed concern for young ecstasy users, since the parts of the brain involved in this kind of memory are not completely developed. "There is some evidence that the frontal cortex is

Does Ecstasy Pose a Psychiatric Danger?

According to the *Psychiatric Times* article "MDMA and Ecstasy," published in February 2002, in a 1998 study of 150 ecstasy users who came forward for substance abuse treatment, 53 percent were diagnosed with a neuropsychiatric problem, or mental illness. A 2000 study that compared heavy and light ecstasy users found that the heavy users had higher levels of paranoia, obsessionality, anxiety, hostility, appetite disturbance, restless sleep, and impulsiveness. But the article goes on to point out several problems with these studies: The subjects are generally abusing other drugs in addition to ecstasy, and the studies generally have no comparison group (in which case it is impossible to conclude that ecstasy is causing the reaction) or a poorly matched comparison group (which can pose the same problem). The studies lack the chemical analyses to identify which drugs are being used, and furthermore, most ecstasy tablets sold to the public have some degree of impurity, containing ketamine, MDA, amphetamine, DXM, or combinations of the above. Any conclusions are thus not scientifically reliable.

still developing in teenagers and adolescents," he said. "If your brain is still developing in parts, there is a strong possibility you could be seriously damaging this development with ecstasy use."[63]

Some research has concluded that ecstasy use is not a cause of memory loss. For example, Charles S. Grob, professor of psychiatry at UCLA School of Medicine, received FDA approval to study MDMA in humans, and ran a study in which he looked at psychological and physical effects in eighteen human volunteers. He found no changes in their memory, and only a few minor blood pressure changes, most occurring in subjects that were on some other form of medication.

While little is known for certain about the permanent effects of ecstasy, these studies certainly suggest to some experts that there are plenty of risks to be concerned about. "Ecstasy damages your brain," says Drew Pinsky, an expert on chemical dependency. "Drugs of abuse, the ones they're choosing to use today, harm your brain, structurally alter—forever—your brain."[64]

▌ Chapter 4

Responding to the Ecstasy Problem

For all the known, suspected, or yet-to-be-identified dangers of using ecstasy, its use has continued to rise. As a result, government officials are continually refining and restructuring their approach to combating ecstasy use. New task forces, intelligence teams, and collaboration between state, local, federal, and international agencies are constantly being created, and prevention programs are constantly evolving. The Drug Enforcement Administration (DEA) oversees a complex network of agents working together with state and local authorities to stop ecstasy trafficking at every stage. But law enforcement officials face some complex challenges as the amount of ecstasy entering the United States skyrockets, the ecstasy trade becomes more violent, and the changing face of the ecstasy dealer makes finding and prosecuting these offenders increasingly difficult.

Supply and Demand

Evidence of an increase in ecstasy use can be seen at America's points of entry. For example, authorities seized just under two hundred ecstasy tablets at all of America's airports in 1993. In 1997 U.S. Customs agents seized five hundred thousand tablets. In 2001 that figure grew to 7.2 million tablets. Experts believe that this increase in the amount of ecstasy entering America is a response to an increase in demand and consumption. In 2002 the DEA estimated that 750,000 tablets of ecstasy were ingested every weekend in New York and New Jersey alone. If trends continue, 1.8 million Americans will have tried ecstasy for the first time in 2004.

Still, compared to other drugs, demand for ecstasy is small. In a June 2000 *Time* magazine article, John Cloud attempted to put the rising ecstasy statistics in perspective:

> Ecstasy remains a niche drug. The number of people who use it once a month remains so small—less than 1% of the population—that ecstasy use doesn't register in the government's drug survey. (By comparison, 5% of Americans older than 12 say they use marijuana once a month, and 1.8% use cocaine.)

Cloud goes on to note, however, "Ecstasy use is growing."[65]

Ecstasy Trafficking

As the seizures of ecstasy at American ports of entry suggest, little of the ecstasy sold in the United States is actually produced there. In fact, the path by which ecstasy enters the United States is long and complicated. The greatest portion of ecstasy sold in the United States is produced in Western Europe, notably the Netherlands and Belgium. Ecstasy is not legal in either of these countries, but despite constant attempts by local law enforcement to crack down on ecstasy production, these nations remain the highest producers of MDMA. The White House Office of Drug Policy estimates that 80 percent of the MDMA consumed worldwide is made in these two countries, largely because the chemicals needed to make ecstasy are more easily available there than in other countries. Dean Boyd, a spokesman for U.S. Customs, told Salon.com, "What Colombia is for cocaine, the Netherlands is for ecstasy."[66] The DEA reports that Poland is becoming a significant producer of ecstasy as well.

Because most ecstasy is produced in Western Europe, distribution was originally controlled by Western European drug traffickers. In recent years, however, organized crime syndicates based in Is-

French customs officials at the port of Calais seize a huge shipment of ecstasy. Most of the ecstasy used in the United States comes from Western Europe.

rael—some composed of Russian émigrés with ties to Russian organized crime syndicates—have forged relationships with these Western European traffickers and taken over much of the drug's distribution. These organized crime units largely recruit American, Israeli, or Western European nationals as couriers to smuggle the drug into America by commercial airlines. In return for a cash payment, these couriers agree to take anywhere from a few to thousands of pills onto the plane with them and smuggle them past U.S. Customs inspectors. Traffickers have also been known to use express mail services. A recent DEA investigation found that thousands of ecstasy pills, in excess of ten thousand per shipment,

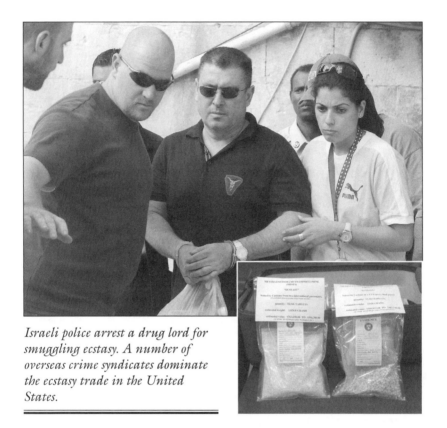

Israeli police arrest a drug lord for smuggling ecstasy. A number of overseas crime syndicates dominate the ecstasy trade in the United States.

were being shipped into the country via one such overnight courier. Ecstasy traffickers also hide quantities of pills in packages and ship them via air freight. Most ecstasy comes to America through the Los Angeles, New York, or Miami airports, where it is then passed on to local distributors.

There is evidence, however, that ever since the terrorist attacks of 9/11, increased airport and border security has hampered smuggling of ecstasy. The apparent result is an increase in the street price of ecstasy and a shift to other drugs, such as painkillers and methamphetamines, by teenagers.

The Changing Face of Ecstasy Dealers

Still, law enforcement efforts to fight ecstasy trafficking have taken on a new urgency as the ecstasy trade has shown signs of becoming violent. Whereas ecstasy was once traded among those attending raves, more recently organized crime has become involved. *Washington Monthly*'s Benjamin Wallace-Wells discussed the expansion of ecstasy sales and the changing face of the drug's dealers:

> In recent years, the ecstasy market has expanded beyond the rave scene, and more sophisticated and dangerous drug organizations have begun to elbow in on what had been mostly a friend-to-friend, white suburban trade. . . . The drug . . . has left the trusting insularity of the rave scene and begun to move out onto the streets, where dealers are more violent, more profit-conscious. . . . Ecstasy, in other words, is becoming a street drug. "We're seeing the same things with ecstasy that we did with cocaine in 1979," says Mark Kleiman, a professor of public policy at UCLA. The user group is expanding, prices are declining, and professional gangs are muscling in.[67]

All of these dealers are attracted to ecstasy by the same thing: money. "With drugs, it's always about the money," says Bridget Brennan, special narcotics prosecutor for New York City. "And dealers are starting to see there is so much money in ecstasy that more people are getting involved, and with that comes more violence."[68]

A Drug Ring Falls

In March 2004 American and Canadian officials worked together to arrest more than 140 people in eighteen cities who formed a drug ring that is estimated to have supplied a full 15 percent of all ecstasy sold in the United States. Importing the pills from the Netherlands via Canada, the group had distributors in virtually every major American city. The leaders were claimed to be Ze Wai Wong, age forty-six, a Chinese man arrested in Toronto, and Mai Phuong Le, thirty-eight, a Vietnamese man arrested in Ottawa. The massive drug bust led to the seizure of more than 500,000 ecstasy pills, 250 ecstasy dyes or stamps, 6 ecstasy pill presses, several handguns, and over $6 million. The ring reportedly took part in some violent incidents, including the killing of a debtor with a meat cleaver in Flushing, Queens. In Eric Lichtblau's April 1, 2004, *New York Times* article "Federal and Canadian Agencies Join in Arresting 140 Said to Supply 15% of U.S. Ecstasy Pills," Deputy Attorney General James B. Comey said that the arrests represented "a top-to-bottom decimation of a dangerous drug organization."

The increasing violence of the ecstasy trade is easy to see. For example, in January 2000 an Israeli ecstasy dealer was found dead at Los Angeles's LAX airport, reportedly killed by two hit men from Israel. Since the incident in Los Angeles, the violence has spread, much as ecstasy has. There have been several ecstasy-related murders in smaller cities like Norfolk, Virginia, and even small towns like Elgin, Illinois, and Valley Stream, New York.

Perhaps not unexpectedly, organized crime has become involved in ecstasy trafficking. In 2002 Salvatore Gravano, a known member of the Mafia, was convicted of running a multimillion-dollar, forty-seven-person ecstasy ring in Arizona. The ring is reported to have used the members of a local white supremacy group, the Devil Dogs, as "muscle." Drug deals were reportedly made behind a restaurant owned by Gravano's wife. Police estimate that the ring made roughly $80,000 on ecstasy sales, and Gravano's take was around $20,000.

Ecstasy Laws

The increasing violence has not only added urgency to law enforcement's effort but also motivated legislators to combat the drug with stricter laws. For example, the Ecstasy Anti-Proliferation Act, sponsored by Senator Bob Graham of Florida, went into effect on May 1, 2001. This law increased the penalties for selling ecstasy to the level of penalties for selling cocaine and heroin. Under this new law, the penalty for trafficking eight hundred or more ecstasy pills is fifteen years in a federal penitentiary.

Another approach has been to try to shut down the venues in which ecstasy is most likely to be used. The so-called RAVE Act (Reducing Americans' Vulnerability to Ecstasy Act), sponsored by Senators Joseph Biden of Delaware and Charles Grassley of Iowa in 2002 was directed at curbing ecstasy use by making party and club promoters legally liable for any drug use that occurs on their premises. The 2002 measure failed in Congress but a revised version of the bill was folded into broad law enforcement legislation in 2003, minus explicit references to raves. Although they might

Mobster Salvatore Gravano was arrested in 2002 for running an ecstasy ring in Arizona. His group resorted to violence and intimidation to corner the local ecstasy market.

not be using the drugs themselves, party and club promoters now face stiff penalties if a patron is caught using ecstasy at their event or facility. Similar laws, which force property owners to keep drugs and drug users off their property, were effective in shutting down the crack houses that plagued urban areas in the 1980s.

Laws against ecstasy are also toughening on the state level. In Georgia, being convicted of having ecstasy pills in one's possession is punishable by two years in prison. In Texas, possession of one gram of MDMA (about four ecstasy pills) leads to two years in prison.

As laws are toughened, however, there is some controversy over the wisdom of trying to reduce the demand for ecstasy this way. Beyond the question of whether harsh penalties deter the sale or use of ecstasy, some contend that the laws may actually be counterproductive. For example, some experts argue that measures such as the RAVE Act may prevent club owners from protecting the safety of those customers who choose to use drugs on the premises. If having water and cool resting places available alerts law enforcement that ecstasy use may be occurring, opponents argue, club owners will stop providing such services, and ecstasy users may die as a result. Grob explains:

> It's certainly unwise. What are they doing? Identifying that chill-out rooms and water are evidence of felonious conduct on the part of the proprietor? All you're going to do is drive the phenomenon further underground, and you're going to make harm-reduction efforts even more difficult to implement than they already are. . . . I think the drug war has yielded catastrophic laws. The laws are compounding the problem because they do not allow for human nature.[69]

Moreover, opponents say, these laws will further crowd America's already-overcrowded prison system with drug users who would benefit more from treatment than from jail time. According to this line of thinking, drug users need help in dealing with their addictions, and that help is generally not available in prison. Many opponents of harsher punishment of ecstasy users argue that placing these generally nonviolent drug users in prison, where they will be forced to learn to survive in a world of violent criminals, can only make them dangerous. As the debate goes on whether these tougher laws actually curb the popularity of ecstasy, many who are combating the drug's use are placing their attention on decreasing demand.

Getting the Word Out

Many believe that one way of curbing ecstasy use is to combat the tendency of users to promote the drug. "There is an evangelical

---

Ecstasy Around the World

In the United States penalties for possessing or selling ecstasy have been made much more harsh in recent years, in line with the penalties for selling or possessing addictive drugs like heroin or crack. Julie Holland's *Ecstasy: The Complete Guide* explains how ecstasy sale and possession is punished around the world.

In Australia ecstasy is classified as a "dangerous drug" under Schedule II of the 1990 Drugs Misuse Act. A conviction for possession of less than half a gram brings two years in prison plus a $1000 (U.S.) fine. Possession of half a gram leads to twenty-five years in jail and a $50,000 (U.S.) fine. Possession of 500 grams or more gets a life sentence.

In Canada ecstasy is classified as a Schedule III drug under the Controlled Drugs and Substances Act of 1997. Importing or trafficking MDMA is punished with a prison term not to exceed ten years. In Canada MDMA possession and sale is punished less harshly than that of cannabis (marijuana) or cocaine.

In China the punishment for possession can range from a prison sentence of less than three years to a sentence of seven years to life, plus a fine. The punishment for trafficking can range from seven years in prison plus a fine to life in prison or even death, plus confiscation of property. In China MDMA is referred to in slang as "head-rocking pills."

Spanish legislation states that MDMA can "cause serious damage to the health." Yet possession of MDMA for personal use (twenty tablets or less) has not been punished since 1986. Trafficking leads to three to nine years in prison and a fine of three times the value of the drugs seized.

In the United Kingdom, possession of MDMA leads to seven years in prison and an unlimited fine. Trafficking of MDMA is punished with life in prison and an unlimited fine.

Punishments for possessing and using MDMA may vary widely across the world, but all of these countries agree that ecstasy is potentially dangerous and should be avoided.

An ecstasy-testing booth at a rave encourages users to test their pills for the presence of harmful contaminants.

fervor with ecstasy," says Robert MacCoun, a University of California, Berkeley, drug policy analyst. "People who experience it tell their friends to buy it."[70] To counter this positive word of mouth, government officials are partnering with various mass media companies to launch campaigns to raise public awareness of the ecstasy problem. The Comcast Corporation, a cable giant, has agreed to donate $51 million worth of advertising time to public service ads urging parents to address the dangers of ecstasy with their children. Comcast reaches over 21 million homes nationwide. The campaign will also use print and outdoor advertisements to direct people to the Web site askyourkidsaboutecstasy.com, where they will find information on the dangers of ecstasy use. John Roberts, the account director of the advertising agency charged with creating the ads, says that the advertisements will stand out because they use satire and direct talk to attract kids' attention. "We see a lot of the antidrug advertising and a lot of it is not always that memorable," he says. "If you're serious about reaching younger people, you really have to do something that isn't just wallpaper."[71]

Harm Reduction

Some experts argue that preventing people from experimenting with drugs is not always possible, since curiosity is part of human nature. These individuals say that the best course is to make certain that those who do take ecstasy are kept as safe as possible. This theory is known as the theory of harm reduction. Bill Hayley, a twenty-eight-year-old from Vancouver, B.C., and a believer in harm reduction, sets up booths at raves where he hands out bottles of water and sells a kit called "E-Z Test," which allows users to test their own ecstasy pills for contaminants that could be even more harmful. Some people oppose this type of assistance on the grounds that it actually encourages clubgoers and ravers to try ecstasy. But Hayley insists that drug experimentation is something some people will engage in no matter what. "You're never going to stop drug use; people are still going to make their choice," he says. "Harm reduction is basically a philosophy or policy that's dedicated to inform or encourage users to make better decisions so they can reduce the risk of harm while they're doing drugs."[72]

One organization has put this philosophy into action. Dance-Safe was founded by Emanuel Sferios and tries to protect dancers at raves and clubs by making certain they are not taking impure or fake ecstasy. DanceSafe representatives set up booths where dancers congregate and offer free tests of pills submitted by the dancers. If the pill is contaminated, the would-be consumer is discouraged from taking it. If the pill is proven to contain MDMA, however, DanceSafe does not interfere if the individual decides to take it. "All drug use has inherent risk, and dance drugs in particular pose certain risks, which are increased by the lack of information,"[73] says Sferios.

Educational Programs

Other experts argue that it is possible to discourage experimentation by sharing the facts about ecstasy. In Seattle, Washington, and surrounding King County, a sweeping educational program was introduced in 2002 to curb the young population's use of ecstasy. After receiving a federal grant of over $336,000 to fight the spread of ecstasy use, public health officials enacted a three-pronged strategy that included 1) taking surveys at places where ecstasy users might congregate, including raves, clubs, youth service centers, and bars, clubs, and bathhouses frequented by gay men; 2) training high school leaders about the effects of club drugs (including ecstasy) as part of the Partners in Prevention project and adding a club-drugs section to antidrug middle school curriculum; and 3) enlisting government agencies, community-based organizations, schools, youths, and adults to review the project's activities, to recommend actions, and to participate in policy development.

"Let me set the record straight. Club drugs and ecstasy are not safe and are not harmless," says King County executive Ron Sims. "As a community, we must get informed about the consequences of these drugs and then support our kids so they can make the best decisions."[74]

Treatment for Ecstasy Dependence

Some experts are focusing their efforts on helping those who have become psychologically dependent on the drug. According to the World Heath Organization, drug dependence is marked by these factors: a strong desire to take the drug, difficulty controlling one's use of the drug, a withdrawal state or unpleasant effects once the drug wears off, developing tolerance, and an increasing neglect of other pleasurable activities and persisting with use despite evidence of harm. Under this definition, ecstasy dependence, while rare, is on the rise.

There are no treatments designed specifically for ecstasy dependence. There is no pharmacological treatment, that is, a harmless alternative to ecstasy. At best, antidepressants such as Zoloft and Paxil may help to counter the depression and lack of energy that some users report following ecstasy use. Generally, treatment for ecstasy dependence involves two steps. According to NIDA, "The most effective treatments for drug abuse and addiction are

Although antidepressants such as Zoloft are effective in rebalancing the serotonin levels of ecstasy users, no specific treatment for MDMA addiction has yet been established.

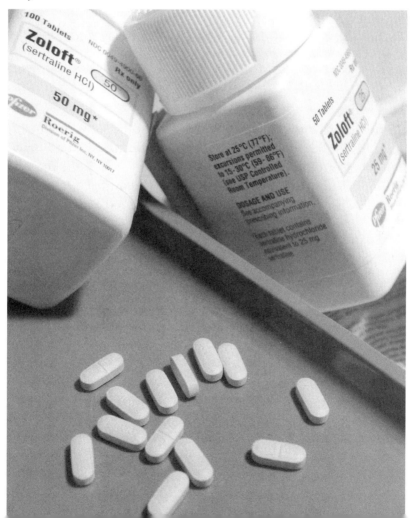

cognitive behavioral interventions that are designed to help modify the patient's thinking, expectancies, and behaviors, and to increase skills in coping with life's stressors."[75] In other words, experts try to change the patterns of thinking and behavior that lead the user to believe he or she needs the drug. The user must stop taking ecstasy, clear his or her body of the drug, and stop putting himself or herself in situations where the temptation to take ecstasy may exist. This is called detoxification and behavior modification.

The second step in treatment for ecstasy dependence is counseling. According to James N. Parker and Philip M. Parker in their book *The Official Patient's Sourcebook on MDMA Dependence:*

> Counseling or behavioral therapies are critical components of effective treatment for addiction. In therapy, patients address issues of motivation, build skills to resist drug use, replace drug-using activities with constructive and rewarding non-drug-using activities, and improve problem-solving abilities. Behavioral therapy also facilitates interpersonal relationships and the individual's ability to function in the family and community.[76]

Ecstasy dependence, then, is a real and growing problem, but experts are confident that they can treat it effectively. At the same time, there are experts who argue that even though the regular, unsupervised use of ecstasy should be discouraged, the drug should be investigated for its potential to do good as well as harm.

Chapter 5

Current Ecstasy Research

Ecstasy's rapid development into a recreational drug led to its being banned for use by psychotherapists, and research into its potential usefulness was never carried out in a scientifically controlled manner. Still, since the beginning of the twenty-first century, while the long-term dangers of ecstasy use are debated, scientists have been granted more chances to study ecstasy as a psychotherapeutic aid than ever before. The goal of these new studies is to learn whether the same effects that motivate clubgoers and others to take ecstasy might make it a useful treatment for crippling psychological disorders.

A Question of Safety

Even though ecstasy is classified by the DEA as a Schedule I (illegal) drug, meaning that it is potentially very dangerous, psychotherapists who administered ecstasy to their patients before it was made illegal insist that it can be used safely in a therapeutic setting. Early proponent George Greer claims that the procedures he and his colleagues followed during the 1970s and 1980s made their patients' use of ecstasy safe. For example, prospective users were interviewed extensively and asked to fill out a long questionnaire.

Based on their responses, patients with existing medical problems were excluded, as were pregnant women. For those patients who were approved for use of MDMA, Greer recalls that the session progressed in this way:

> We started with 75 to 125 mg, and the person could tell us that they wanted a low, medium, or high dose within that range. An hour and a half to two hours later, we would offer them an additional 50 mg, and most would take it. . . . We would be with the person for six to eight hours. The first two to three hours the person would listen to music with headphones, lying down and wearing eyeshades. During the second three-hour period the person would start talking and interacting with us and doing something more like psychotherapy. We would talk about problems and issues and work through difficult feelings. When we thought that the person could take care of themselves and the emotional processing was complete, we would leave.[77]

Anecdotal Evidence

For all the care therapists might have used in administering MDMA, they still did not keep the kind of records or structure their experiments in a way that allowed impartial evaluation of their results. In the absence of controlled studies proving ecstasy's potential therapeutic benefits, those who want to study ecstasy or loosen the restrictions on its use rely instead on anecdotal evidence of the drug's usefulness. At the very least, however, many credit the drug with speeding up the process of psychotherapy. "For most people the heightened and deepened states of awareness facilitated by the drug serves as a kind of preview, as it were, a taste of the possibilities that exist for much greater emotional openness and relatedness than they had imagined,"[78] claim therapists Ralph Metzner and Sophia Adamson. The role of MDMA in psychotherapy is "to make the therapy go deeper and go faster and be less uncomfortable," according to physician Julie Holland. "MDMA is the only anti-anxiety medicine that isn't sedating. And that makes it unique and useful to psychiatry."[79]

Ecstasy calms patients and allows them to confront their deepest problems. Holland says that MDMA makes patients more secure and less defensive: "All the defenses are stripped away, replaced by courage to take a thorough inventory and share what is found."[80]

Some psychotherapists claim that ecstasy can actually accelerate the psychotherapeutic process in their patients.

Holland claims that there are four basic ways in which ecstasy can aid psychotherapy: connection, recall, insight, and acceptance. First, she claims that MDMA can facilitate the connection between patient and therapist. Patients must trust their therapists and believe that the therapist truly has the best intentions. With its empathetic effects, ecstasy allows the user to form this bond more quickly than usual. Patients feel safe and trusting. In a 1990 study done on avowed users, G.R. Greer and R. Tolbert found that, under the influence of MDMA, "Patients experience a state of reduced defensiveness that promotes self-disclosure and trust for several hours after ingestion, thereby strengthening the therapeutic alliance."[81]

Recall

During times of great stress or trauma, people sometimes "forget" specific incidents, particularly those which cause the most pain. During treatment, the therapist may seek to uncover these repressed memories and force patients to deal with the underlying fear or pain that may be causing problems in their daily lives. This

Ecstasy as an Antidepressant?

As ecstasy grows in popularity, experts are becoming increasingly concerned that some people who suffer from clinical depression may use ecstasy to self-medicate, leading to psychological addiction. In the *New York Times* January 21, 2001, article "Experiencing Ecstasy," Matthew Klam describes ecstasy as "a whopper of an antidepressant. Whereas most antidepressants keep your brain from emptying reservoirs of serotonin too quickly, ecstasy floods your brain with the stuff." The problems with treating depression with ecstasy are numerous, including the fact that it is an illegal drug, and that little is known about the long-term effects of frequent uses. Clinically depressed people who use ecstasy to feel better could easily end up psychologically dependent on the drug. It is far more advisable to see a therapist and discuss a milder, legal antidepressant.

Using ecstasy as an antidepressant presents a number of dangers, including the risk of psychological addiction to the drug.

can often be a long and difficult process. MDMA, advocates claim, helps patients access repressed memories, and react to them with a minimum of anxiety and stress. Metzner and Adamson cite an example of a rape victim who has amnesia regarding her attack but who was suddenly able to recall and discuss the trauma of the incident while under the influence of ecstasy:

> [MDMA] . . . took me back into the experience of the attack that was too much for my psyche to bear. During the experience with Adam [ecstasy], I moved in and out of the attack. . . . It has seemed that Adam has allowed me to . . . re-experience what I needed to re-experience, and to desensitize myself to my surroundings.[82]

Often, the experiences recalled during an ecstasy session had been completely forgotten. Swiss psychiatrist Marianne Bloch remembers one of these experiences with a couple of her patients: "With one patient . . . it brought back this incest problem, with another it brought back very early childhood memories that as a child he had been sick very often, which he had forgotten. The emotional stuff of childhood came up, and he relived it again."[83] Psychotherapists claim that not only does MDMA promote recall of repressed memories, but that the patient is able to remember what was discussed, and thus the progress that was made, after the session is over. This, therapists say, is not always the case with other types of therapy, such as hypnosis.

In addition to recalling repressed memories, psychotherapists claim, patients under the influence of ecstasy are better able to gain a sense of closure regarding the past. Marcela Ot'alora, a rape victim who underwent therapy with MDMA in 1984, experienced this insight when she reached an important emotional milestone after taking ecstasy during a session: "I think for the first time in my life I was able to have compassion for myself, and also felt I was strong enough to face something that was frightening without falling apart. . . . It allows you to go into the trauma and know it is past, and separate it from the present."[84]

Once the memory is recalled, psychotherapists claim that MDMA-assisted patients are better able to come to terms with their memories and issues than those who undergo conventional therapy. Metzner and Adamson bring up the experience of one patient, a victim of sexual abuse, who experienced such acceptance:

> Reliving this incident helped to free up my energy and emotions in a number of ways. It feels as though this process will be ongoing for some time. In general, my journey with Adam [ecstasy] affirmed who I am, what I am doing, where I am going. . . . I am able to perceive, receive, and respond to love in a much more open way than I did a few weeks ago.[85]

Although ecstasy is most commonly used to enhance the club experience, some researchers believe the drug holds great therapeutic potential in clinical environments.

Set and Setting

Most psychotherapists agree that "set" and "setting" are extremely important in the outcome of any experience with a psychoactive drug like MDMA. Metzner and Adamson define set as the patient's expectations, intention, attitude, and personality, and setting as the physical and social context, presence, and attitude of others, including the therapist. In other words, the expectations of the user and the environment in which the drug is taken significantly affect the outcome of the experience. This is why, while many psychiatrists believe that ecstasy is safe in therapeutic contexts, few would argue for its wholesale legalization. "Those who take the drug 'for recreation' or 'just to experience the high' are likely to get just that: a pleasant, even pleasurable, few hours, with little or no intellectual insight,"[86] say Metzner and Adamson. In the proper setting, however, great improvements can be made, according to Dr. Mark Kleiman. He claims that anecdotal evidence implies that ecstasy can make people better able to deal with their circumstances:

> I've never heard people say to me "methamphetamine improved my life, I'm a better person for having used methamphetamine." Same thing with cocaine. I know people who like to use cocaine but I've never heard anybody try to claim "cocaine is good for me." MDMA, lots of people think this drug improved their life, and continued to think that after they stopped using it.[87]

Risks of Use in Psychotherapy

While all medical professionals are aware of the inherent risks in taking MDMA, some believe that MDMA can be used safely in a clinical setting. Holland agrees:

> I am not coming out and saying ecstasy is safe. What I am saying is that a single dose of MDMA—known MDMA—when you're not dancing and overhydrating but when you're sitting in an office with a psychiatrist, talking about therapeutic material, that is relatively safe. . . . In a therapeutic model, you know what you're taking, you're taking a very small amount and you're taking it once or twice in your lifetime and that's it. That is safe.[88]

Some therapists say that MDMA is most remarkable for the lack of danger it poses to healthy people and that it is nonaddictive, physically or psychologically, when taken in a therapeutic setting. Physician and news commentator Drew Pinsky accepts that MDMA may be beneficial in cases where patients do not respond to conventional therapy, but warns that it is still a powerful and potentially dangerous drug:

> People need to not become confused about the danger of drugs and their potential therapeutic value, understand there are some very dangerous medications like morphine or Oxycontin that are tremendously powerful and important medications. And here is an example of a medication, ecstasy, which we know has some addictive potential. We know it's potentially a neurotoxin. We know people can get hyperthermia and die from even as much as one exposure. And yet there is a growing sort of body of evidence that there may be some therapeutic value for this drug in desperate situations.[89]

In recent years, some psychotherapists have been given special permission to run controlled studies on the effects of ecstasy in psychotherapy. According to Mark Kleiman, director of the Drug Policy Analysis Program at UCLA, "There's obviously been a significant shift at the regulatory agencies and the Institutional Review Boards. There are studies being approved that wouldn't have been approved 10 years ago. And there are studies being proposed that wouldn't have been proposed 10 years ago."[90]

Swiss Research

The first such studies took place in Switzerland in the late 1980s. In 1988 the Swiss Federal Office for Public Health allowed several therapists in private practice to use MDMA in their therapeutic research. Today researchers at the Psychiatric University Hospital in Zurich continue to experiment with MDMA in controlled, therapeutic settings.

A group of Swiss psychiatrists tracked the progress of their patients who used MDMA in psychotherapy sessions between 1988 and 1993. A total of 121 patients were involved; altogether they took part in 818 sessions. The patients remained in psychotherapy for an average of three years. When the patients were evaluated in 1993, 65 percent deemed themselves significantly improved and an additional 26 percent deemed themselves slightly improved. Many patients reported improved self-acceptance, self-esteem, and reduced levels of fear and other health complaints. Sixty-five percent claimed that their MDMA-enhanced sessions were very important emotionally, 56 percent said the sessions were very important to their interpersonal relationships, and 49 percent cited important insights about their own lives. And 84 percent of patients claimed that their quality of life had improved. Virtually no patients reported an increased use of drugs after the therapy; in fact, a substantial number of patients said that their use of drugs had decreased.

Dr. Drew Pinsky has conceded the therapeutic value of ecstasy, but he warns that it is still a very dangerous drug.

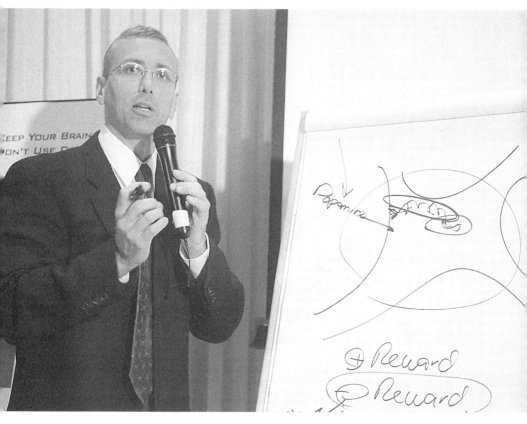

Samuel Widmer, who oversaw the various psychotherapists allowed to administer MDMA in private practice, characterizes their research in this way:

> We have not observed any negative effects, neither of a psychological or physical kind. No addictions to MDMA have been observed after use of MDMA. To the contrary, we have been able to confirm that other addictions (alcohol, medical drugs, heroin, etc.) were greatly reduced by MDMA-supported therapy.[91]

Post-Traumatic Stress Disorder

The characteristics of ecstasy of promoting recall, insight, and acceptance made researchers wonder how the drug might benefit patients of post-traumatic stress disorder. Post-traumatic stress disorder (PTSD) is a condition common to those who have experienced life-threatening events or witnessed particularly shocking incidents. It is marked by nightmares, the urge to physically harm

The ability of ecstasy to promote recall, insight, and acceptance of painful memories may prove useful in the treatment of post-traumatic stress disorder.

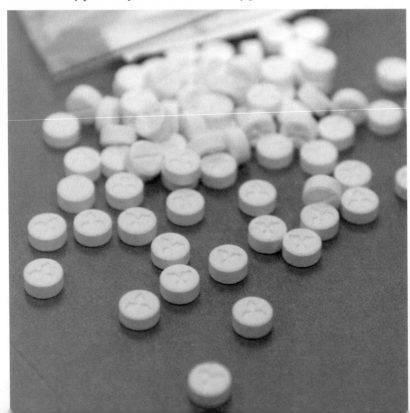

oneself, and extreme anxiety. Common symptoms of PTSD include depression, loss of self-esteem, feelings of guilt, avoidance behavior in interpersonal relations, expression deficits, and sexual problems. Sufferers often struggle with substance abuse as well. Researchers wondered whether ecstasy's ability to help patients recall and deal with repressed memories might prove beneficial to sufferers of PTSD.

In 2001 headlines were made when the Spanish government gave researcher Jose Carlos Bouso the go-ahead to perform a clinical study on the effectiveness of MDMA in treating PTSD. "The main objectives in treating PTSD are to confront the trauma and help the victim regain self-esteem and a sense of security,"[92] Bouso says. George Greer claims that the trauma experienced by PTSD sufferers becomes locked in the brain, and that MDMA opens the door to recalling that trauma while also suppressing the fear and anxiety associated with those memories. Able to recall and process the trauma, the PTSD sufferer can return to normal life.

Holland compares MDMA to mental anesthesia: "[Therapeutic MDMA] is like anesthesia during surgery. . . . It really lets the procedure unfold in a way that's not nearly as uncomfortable for the patient. It allows it to go deeper and get more of the malignant material out."[93] Bouso claims that 50 to 60 percent of victims of sexual assault suffer from post-traumatic stress disorder. Rape victims experience fear, anxiety, vulnerability, stress, and confusion, which can become chronic. Bouso believes that, given MDMA's ability to give access to painful memories and encourage acceptance, the drug would be an effective treatment for people who have experienced sexual assault. He explains that MDMA benefits the patient by creating a subjective sense of well-being in which the patient's defenses disappear. This allows the patient to discuss and analyze deeply held feelings, to reexperience the traumatic event without anxiety.

On February 24, 2004, headlines were made in the United States when the DEA issued researcher Michael Mithoefer of South Carolina a Schedule I license to legally obtain ecstasy in order to test its effectiveness in treating PTSD. This was the first approval granted by the DEA to study ecstasy as a therapeutic aid. "We owe it to [sufferers of PTSD]," said Mithoefer. "It would be irresponsible for the medical community not to investigate something like this."[94]

To qualify for the study, twenty potential subjects must be victims of assaults unrelated to combat, must have moderate to severe PTSD that is unresponsive to other drugs, and must undergo preliminary therapy sessions with Mithoefer. Then each will spend the first session talking, listening to music, and lying on a couch as required. Each patient must discuss his or her trauma at some point. Twelve of the patients will be treated with MDMA, whereas eight will receive a placebo, a sugar pill that looks identical to the MDMA tablet. Neither the subjects nor their doctors will be told which patients are getting the real drug. This is what is known as a "double blind" study, and helps ensure against the doctors unintentionally interacting differently with the patients who actually receive the drug. Many advocates of MDMA-assisted therapy have high hopes for the Mithoefer study. They hope that if Mithoefer gets encouraging results, the DEA may allow more MDMA research in the future.

Not everyone is so enthusiastic about the Mithoefer study. Scott Lillienfeld, a psychiatrist at Emory University, questions the validity of such studies or of the use of MDMA in therapy in general. He wonders whether any progress made under the influence of a drug can be true and lasting, claiming that Mithoefer's hypothesis is "at the least, muddled. . . . If you're calm, you're not getting to the root of the problem."[95] He believes that getting to the root of a problem involves facing the trauma head-on, not under the influence of a drug. And most psychotherapists are quick to admit that these kinds of insights are certainly reachable without the help of MDMA. It is the speed and relative painlessness of these insights under the influence of MDMA that excites the advocates of its therapeutic use.

Ecstasy Research and the Future

Looking forward, many psychotherapists hope that MDMA will help patients with a variety of problems, including depression,

MDMA and Spirituality

MDMA has also become popular among people hoping to make spiritual breakthroughs. According to Ralph Metzner and Sophia Adamson in Holland's *Ecstasy: The Complete Guide*, "Experiences of spiritual enlightenment and of discovery are commonplace in the accounts of MDMA experiences." It is believed MDMA's ability to make the user feel secure and happy encourages spiritual awakening. One user recalls: "I allow, invite, surrender God into my own body. God consciousness aches for and eagerly awaits this moment to enter me, as it longs to enter each of us, at any and every moment." Another user recalls "an awareness of being here, beyond here. . . . I remember . . . [that] the heart [is] always restless until it finds rest in God. I feel that complete rest, no searching, finally home."

schizophrenia, and even painful terminal illnesses. They hope that MDMA's ability to facilitate connection, recall and insight, and acceptance could help patients deal with a wide variety of issues. Jane Riedlinger and Michael Montagne are excited about the drug's possible role in treating depression, claiming that MDMA's ability to stimulate positive feelings such as openness and empathy could help such patients. Those who experience depression so severe that they contemplate suicide might particularly benefit, because such individuals often feel intensely isolated:

> Many cases seem to be manifestations of alienation. The anguish of the suicidal person is frequently that of a person in exile. He or she feels totally isolated, singled out by fate to suffer hardships and endless frustration alone. Such people often find it hard to deal with the conflicts and demands of interpersonal relationships. They withdraw into a private, lonely world. . . . By providing relief from overwhelmingly dark emotions, MDMA likely can help forestall the act of suicide or otherwise alleviate the patient's sense of hopelessness. This buys time for the drug's second major effect, facilitating psychotherapy by helping to enhance the patient's trust and by inviting self-analysis and disclosure.[96]

Holland proposes that MDMA may be an effective treatment for people with schizophrenia, an illness in which an overproduction of dopamine causes sufferers to experience overwhelming sensory input, including hearing voices, seeing terrifying visions, or—in some cases—detecting conspiracies where none are present. Holland points out that MDMA's chemical functions may help stem the tide of dopamine in a schizophrenia patient's brain. She says that the serotonin system seems to inhibit dopamine production, so ecstasy, which stimulates the serotonin system, may be an effective antipsychotic drug.

As psychotherapists wait for the outcome of the Mithoefer study and to learn whether the DEA might allow these new hypotheses to be tested, psychiatrist John Halpern of Harvard Medical School won government approval in December 2004 to run a trial testing the effectiveness of MDMA in relieving anxiety among terminal cancer patients. It is believed that, because ecstasy is so effective at allowing psychotherapy patients to discuss difficult subjects, the drug may be helpful in allowing terminal cancer patients to deal with issues of mortality, anger, and helplessness. Privately some cancer patients have already experimented with MDMA as a means of facilitating discussions with loved ones. Cloud reports on one such couple in *Time* magazine:

> Sue and Shane Stevens have sent the three kids away for the weekend. They have locked the doors and hidden the car so no one will bug them. Tonight they hope to talk about Shane's cancer, a topic they have mostly avoided for years. It has eaten away at their marriage just as it corrodes his kidney. A friend has recommended that they take ecstasy, except he calls it MDMA and says therapists used it 20 years ago to get people to discuss difficult topics. And, in fact, after tonight, Sue and Shane will open up, and Sue will come to believe MDMA is prolonging her marriage—and perhaps Shane's life.[97]

Not every psychotherapist is as optimistic about the use of MDMA in treating anxiety in cancer patients. Vivian Rakoff, emeritus professor of psychiatry at the University of Toronto, remains skeptical that this is a wonder drug, pointing out that this is hardly the first time a single drug has been believed to hold the secret to quickly reaching the unconscious: "The notion of the revelatory moment due to some drug or maneuver that will allow you to change your life has been around for a long time. Every

Some scientists hope that ecstasy may one day help to treat such psychoses as schizophrenia.

few years, something comes along that claims to be what [famed psychotherapist Sigmund] Freud called the 'royal road to the unconscious.'"[98] Steven Hyman, professor of neurobiology at Harvard Medical School and former director of the National Institute of Mental Health, agrees with Lillienfeld that any progress made under the influence of a drug is not real progress: "If you asked me to place a bet, I would be skeptical. In general, one worries

These ecstasy tablets were seized by U.S. Customs officials. Some people hope that ecstasy may one day be a legal, doctor-prescribed drug.

that insights gained under states of disinhibition or mild euphoria or different cognitive states with illusions may seem strange and distant from the vantage of our ordinary life."[99] But all agree that the only objective way to measure the effectiveness of ecstasy as a psychotherapeutic aid is by performing more research.

For his part, Alexander Shulgin, the man who first synthesized MDMA and distributed it to his psychotherapist friends, hopes that MDMA-assisted psychotherapy is soon a legal reality. "My hope is that it be relocated from a legal and criminal arena to the medical and personal arena—that it be removed from legal control and be placed in personal control,"[100] he says. It remains to be seen whether the law will agree.

Notes

Introduction: A Growing Problem

1. Quoted in Jessica Reaves, "The Pill That Has Parents in a Panic," *Time*, April 3, 2000. www.time.com/time/nation/article/0,8599,42405,00.html
2. Quoted in Fox Butterfield, "Violence Rises as Club Drug Spreads Out into the Streets," *New York Times*, June 24, 2001.

Chapter 1: Ecstasy Arrives

3. Quoted in Drake Bennett, "Dr. Ecstasy," *The New York Times*, January 30, 2005.
4. Quoted in Bennett, "Dr. Ecstasy."
5. Quoted in Bennett, "Dr. Ecstasy."
6. Quoted in Gerald Valentine, "MDMA and Ecstasy," *Psychiatric Times*, February 2002. www.psychiatrictimes.com/p020246.html.
7. Quoted in Paul Glanzrock, "A Dose of Generation X," *Psychology Today*, May/June 1994, p. 16.
8. Quoted in Bennett, "Dr. Ecstasy."
9. Dawn MacKeen, "The Big E," Salon.com, July 7, 1999. www.dir.salon.com/health/feature/1999/07/07/ecstasy/index.html?sid=136202.
10. Quoted in Jerome Beck and Marsha Rosenbaum, *Pursuit of Ecstasy: The MDMA Experience*, Albany: State University of New York Press, 1994, p. 64.
11. Beck and Rosenbaum, *Pursuit of Ecstasy*, p. 66.

12. Bruce Eisner, *Ecstasy: The MDMA Story*, Berkeley, CA: Ronin, 1994, p. 34.

13. Matthew Klam, "Experiencing Ecstasy," *New York Times*, January 21, 2001.

14. Quoted in Beck and Rosenbaum, *Pursuit of Ecstasy*, p. 70.

15. Quoted in PBS, "In the Mix: Ecstasy." www.pbs.org/inthemix/shows/show_ecstasy.html

16. Anonymous, "Dizziness, Panic Attacks, and Therapeutic Use." www.ecstasy.org/experiences/trip103.html.

17. Karl Jansen, "Nocturnal Panic Attack." Ecstasy.org, http://ecstasy.org/qanda/q7.html.

18. Jansen, "Nocturnal Panic Attack."

19. Bangfrog, "Disintegration, Anxiety and Meltdown," Erowid.org. www.erowid.org/experiences/exp.php?ID=2445.

20. Beck and Rosenbaum, *Pursuit of Ecstasy*, p. 106.

21. Liz O'Brien, "The Agony After Ecstasy," Salon.com, June 14, 2000. http://dir.salon.com/health/feature/2000/06/14/ecstasy/index.html?sid=836931.

22. Quoted in Mary Spicuzza, "Nightly Grind," *Metro*, March 23, 2000. www.metroactive.com/papers/metro/03.23.00/ecstasy1-0012.html.

23. O'Brien, "The Agony After Ecstasy."

24. Klam, "Experiencing Ecstasy."

25. Quoted in Paul R. Robbins, *Hallucinogens*. Springfield, NJ: Enslow, 1996, p. 36.

Chapter 2: The Evolving Ecstasy Scene

26. Quoted in Julie Holland, ed. *Ecstasy: The Complete Guide*. Rochester, VT: Park Street, 2001, p. 13.

27. Quoted in Beck and Rosenbaum, *The Pursuit of Ecstasy*, p. 19.

28. Push and Mireille Silcott, *The Book of E: All About Ecstasy*. London: Omnibus, 2000, p. 14.

29. Silcott, *The Book of E*, p. 16.

30. Quoted in Silcott, *The Book of E*, p. 5.

31. Quoted in Silcott, *The Book of E*, p. 19.

32. Quoted in Silcott, *The Book of E*, p. 18.

33. Quoted in Holland, *Ecstasy*, p. 226.

34. Quoted in Bob Woodruff, "Ecstasy and Therapy," ABC News, April 1, 2004. www.abcnews.com/sections/ WNT/Primetime/Ecstasy_therapy_040401.html.

35. Quoted in Klam, "Experiencing Ecstasy."

36. Simon Reynolds, *Generation Ecstasy*. New York: Little, Brown, 1998, p.84.

37. Quoted in John Cloud, "The Lure of Ecstasy," *Time*, June 5, 2000. www.time.com/time/europe/magazine/2000/ 0717/cover.html.

38. Jessica Reaves, "The Pill That Has Parents in a Panic," *Time*, April 3, 2000.

39. Quoted in Office of National Drug Control Policy, "*Pulse Check* Trends in Drug Abuse Mid-Year 2000," *Pulse Check*. www.whitehousedrugpolicy.gov/publications/drugfact/ pulsechk/midyear2000/clubdrugs.html.

40. Cloud, "The Lure of Ecstasy."

Chapter 3: The Dangers of Ecstasy

41. Quoted in Cloud, "The Lure of Ecstasy."

42. Michele Spiess, "MDMA (Ecstasy)," Office of National Drug Control Policy, February 2004. www.whitehouse drugpolicy.gov/publications/factsht/mdma/index.html.

43. Quoted in Holland, *Ecstasy*, p. 74.

44. Klam, "Experiencing Ecstasy."

45. Benjamin Wallace-Wells, "The Agony of Ecstasy," *Washington Monthly*, May 2003. www.washingtonmonthly.com/features/2003/0305.wallace-wells.html.
46. Quoted in Silcott, *The Book of E*, p. 120.
47. Donald G. McNeil Jr., "Research on Ecstasy is Clouded by Errors," *The New York Times*, December 2, 2003.
48. Quoted in McNeil, "Research on Ecstasy is Clouded by Errors."
49. Quoted in McNeil, "Research on Ecstasy is Clouded by Errors."
50. Reynolds, *Generation Ecstasy*, p. 86.
51. Quoted in Michele Spiess, "MDMA (Ecstasy)."
52. Quoted in CBS, "Perfect Little Girl," *48 Hours*, CBS News, July 26, 2001. www.cbsnews.com/stories/2000/11/28/48hours/main252811.shtml.
53. DanceSafe, "What Is Ecstasy?" http://dancesafe.org/documents/druginfo/ecstasy.php.
54. Quoted in MacKeen, "The Big E."
55. Quoted in CBS, "Perfect Little Girl."
56. Quoted in MacKeen, "The Big E."
57. Quoted in MacKeen, "The Big E."
58. Quoted in Erowid, "Summary and Review of *Ecstasy Rising*, an ABC News report," Erowid.org, April 2004. www.erowid.org/chemicals/mdma/mdma_media1.shtml.
59. Valentine, "MDMA and Ecstasy."
60. Quoted in National Institute on Drug Abuse, "Long-Term Brain Injury From Use of Ecstasy." www.nida.nih.gov/MedAdv/99/NR-614b.html.
61. Quoted in Eric Nagourney, "Vital Signs: Consequences: Memory Often a Victim of Ecstasy," *New York Times*, April 10, 2001.

62. Quoted in Gerard Seenan, "Regular Ecstasy Users Risking Loss of Memory," *Guardian Unlimited*, March 29, 2001. http://society.guardian.co.uk/drugsandalcohol/story/0,8150,464981,00.html.

63. Quoted in Seenan, "Regular Ecstasy Users Risking Loss of Memory."

64. Quoted in CBS, "The Heroin of the Heartland," cbs news.com, July 31, 2002. www.cbsnews.com/stories/2002/01/31/health/main326497.shtml.

Chapter 4: Responding to the Ecstasy Problem

65. Cloud, "The Lure of Ecstasy."

66. Quoted in MacKeen, "The Big E."

67. Wallace-Wells, "The Agony of Ecstasy."

68. Quoted in Butterfield, "Violence Rises as Club Drug Spreads Out into the Streets."

69. Quoted in Sheerly Avni, "Ecstasy Begets Empathy," Salon.com, September 12, 2002. www.salon.com/mwt/feature/2002/09/12/grob_interview/index.html.

70. Quoted in Erowid, "Summary and Review of *Ecstasy Rising*, an ABC News report."

71. Quoted in Nat Ives, "A Big Donation of Time and Space to Fight the Drug Ecstasy," *New York Times*, October 16, 2003.

72. Quoted in MacKeen, "The Big E."

73. Quoted in Ted Oehmke, "The War on Information," Salon.com, June 15, 2000. http://dir.salon.com/health/feature/2000/06/15/ecstasy_bill/index.html?sid-833331.

74. Quoted in King County, "Public Health Joined by Local and National Partners in Ecstasy Education Campaign," Public Health (Seattle and King County), February 14, 2002. www.metrokc.gov/HEALTH/news/02021401.htm.

75. Quoted in Office of National Drug Control Policy, "Research Report Series—MDMA Abuse (Ecstasy)," National Institute on Drug Abuse. www.drugabuse.gov/Research Reports/MDMA/MDMA5.html#preventing.

76. James N. Parker and Philip M. Parker, *The Official Patient's Sourcebook on MDMA Dependence*. San Diego, CA: ICON Group International, 2002, p. 21.

Chapter 5: Current Ecstasy Research

77. Quoted in Holland, *Ecstasy*, p. 231.

78. Quoted in Holland, *Ecstasy*, p. 185.

79. Quoted in Jonathan Darman, "Out of the Club, onto the Couch," *Newsweek*, December 5, 2003. www.maps.org/media/newsweekonline120503.html.

80. Holland, *Ecstasy*, p. 178.

81. Quoted in Valentine, "MDMA and Ecstasy."

82. Quoted in Holland, *Ecstasy*, p. 188.

83. Quoted in Nicholas Saunders, "E for Ecstasy," Ecstasy.org, May 1993. www.ecstasy.org/books/e4x/.

84. Quoted in Rick Weiss, "DEA Approves Trial Use of Ecstasy in Trauma Cases," *Washington Post*, March 2, 2004, www.maps.org/pipermail/maps_forum/2004-March/0059 84.html.

85. Quoted in Holland, *Ecstasy*, p. 187.

86. Quoted in Holland, *Ecstasy*, p. 186.

87. Quoted in Erowid, "Summary and Review of *Ecstasy Rising*, an ABC News report."

88. Quoted in Darman, "Out of the Club, onto the Couch."

89. Quoted in CNN, "'Ecstasy' Benefit?" *American Morning*, February 26, 2004. http://transcripts.cnn.com/TRAN SCRIPTS/0402/26/ltm.19.html.

90. Quoted in Bennett, "Dr. Ecstasy."

91. Quoted in Kevin Durrheim, "Therapists on E," *New Therapist*. www.newtherapist.com/therape.html.

92. Quoted in Holland, *Ecstasy*, p. 252.

93. Quoted in Darman, "Out of the Club, onto the Couch."

94. Quoted in Darman, "Out of the Club, onto the Couch."

95. Quoted in "Ecstasy Approved for Medical Study," cnn.com, February 25, 2004.

96. Quoted in Holland, *Ecstasy*, pp. 268–71.

97. John Cloud, "The Lure of Ecstasy."

98. Quoted in Bennett, "Dr. Ecstasy."

99. Quoted in Bennett, "Dr. Ecstasy."

100. Quoted in Holland, *Ecstasy*, p. 65.

Organizations
to Contact

DanceSafe
536 4th Street, Oakland, CA 94609
Web site: www.dancesafe.org

DanceSafe is a nonprofit, harm reduction organization promoting health and safety within the rave and nightclub community. It is dedicated to harm reduction and educating drug users about the potential risks of ecstasy. Its Web site features useful information on ecstasy and many other drugs.

Drug Enforcement Administration (DEA)
2401 Jefferson Davis Hwy., Alexandria, VA 22301
phone: (202) 307-8846
Web site: www.usdoj.gov/dea/indesx.htm

The Drug Enforcement Administration is the arm of federal law enforcement charged with keeping illegal drugs out of the country and off the streets. The DEA is very helpful in supplying information about the status and trafficking of illegal drugs in the United States.

National Institute on Drug Abuse (NIDA)
6001 Executive Blvd., Room 5213, Bethesda, MD 20892-9651
phone: (301) 443-1124
Web site: www.nida.nih.gov

NIDA has extensive up-to-date information about drug abuse in the United States. Dedicated to warning the public of the risks of drug abuse, NIDA supplies research findings, statistics, and general information on various drugs.

For Further Reading

Books

James Barter, *Hallucinogens*. San Diego: Lucent Books, 2002. Although this book deals with a broad class of drugs, it does include a discussion of ecstasy.

Nicholas Saunders and Rick Doblin, *Ecstasy: Dance, Trance & Transformation*. San Francisco: Quick Trading, 1996. Filled with first-person accounts, this book by two experts in the field covers important issues related to ecstasy.

Brock E. Schroeder, David J. Triggle, and Brook Schroeder, *Ecstasy* (Drugs: The Straight Facts). Broomall, PA: Chelsea House, 2004. A well-written overview of the drug aimed at younger readers.

Myra Weatherly. *Ecstasy and Other Designer Drugs*. Springfield, NJ: Enslow, 2000. Aimed at young adults, this book is an excellent source of information about the drug.

Web Sites

Ecstasy.org (www.ecstasy.org). This Web site is dedicated to disseminating information about ecstasy research, use, and risks.

EMedicine (www.emedicine.com) A Web site with useful information aimed at health professionals, but it has much helpful information about the effects of ecstasy.

Multidisciplinary Association for Psychedelic Studies (MAPS) (www.maps.org). A nonprofit research and educational organizations, MAPS sponsors scientific research designed to develop psychedelics and marijuana into FDA-approved prescription medicines, and to educate the public about the risks and benefits of these drugs. Its Web site contains useful, up-to-date information about ecstasy research.

The Vaults of Erowid (www.erowid.org) This Web site, dedicated to "documenting the complex relationship between humans and psychoactives," provides useful answers to frequently asked questions and firsthand accounts of experiences of ecstasy users.

Works Consulted

Books

Jerome Beck and Marsha Rosenbaum, *Pursuit of Ecstasy: The MDMA Experience*. Albany: State University of New York Press, 1994. This book does an excellent job of tracing the emergence of ecstasy in the 1970s and 1980s and the effects of the drug. It is, unfortunately, somewhat out of date and does not cover current use.

Bruce Eisner, *Ecstasy: The MDMA Story*. Berkeley, CA: Ronin, 1994. This book provides an overview of the drug's effects and history, though it does not cover the drug's recent explosion in popularity.

Richard Hammersley, Furzana Khan, and Jason Ditton, *Ecstasy and the Rise of the Chemical Generation*. London: Routledge, 2002. This book details a study of ecstasy users done in the United Kingdom. It features many first-person experiences and discusses the reasons people take the drug.

Julie Holland, ed. *Ecstasy: The Complete Guide*. Rochester, VT: Park Street, 2001. An excellent collection of writings by experts in the field, this book is an exhaustive and up-to-date overview of the drug.

Cynthia Kuhn, Scott Swartzwelder, and Wilkie Wilson, *Buzzed: The Straight Facts About the Most Used and Abused Drugs from Alcohol to Ecstasy*. New York: W. W. Norton, 2003. This book provides brief, information-packed overviews of the effects and risks of various recreational drugs.

James N. Parker and Philip M. Parker, *The Official Patient's Sourcebook on MDMA Dependence*. San Diego, CA: ICON Group International, 2002. This is a useful guide for searching out information on ecstasy dependence and treatment both in print and on the Internet.

Paul R. Robbins, *Hallucinogens*. Springfield, NJ: Enslow, 1996. An overview of hallucinogenic drugs, one of the two classes of drugs that ecstasy falls into.

Push and Mirielle Silcott, *The Book of E: All About Ecstasy*. London: Omnibus, 2000. This book provides an excellent overview of the history of ecstasy as a recreational drug and how it has effected society.

Simon Reynolds, *Generation Ecstasy*. New York: Little, Brown and Company, 1998. This book is a discussion of rave culture and techno music, but there is some useful information about ecstasy and its use in raves.

Periodicals

Winda Benedetti, "Ecstasy Supporters Hope FDA-Approved Study Will Vindicate Drug," *The Seattle Post-Intelligencer*, May 9, 2002.

Drake Bennett, "Dr. Ecstasy," *New York Times*, January 30, 2005.

Fox Butterfield, "Violence Rises as Club Drug Spreads Out into the Streets," *New York Times*, June 24, 2001.

Erika Check, "The Ups and Downs of Ecstasy," *Nature*, May 13, 2004.

Alan Feuer, "Distilling the Truth in the Ecstasy Buzz: Much Talk, and Dissent, on Drug's Rise," *New York Times*, August 6, 2000.

Paul Glanzrock, "A Dose of Generation X," *Psychology Today*, May/June 1994.

Nat Ives, "A Big Donation of Time and Space to Fight the Drug Ecstasy," *New York Times*, October 16, 2003.

Matthew Klam, "Experiencing Ecstasy," *New York Times*, January 21, 2001.

Eric Lichtblau, "Federal and Canadian Agencies Join in Arresting 140 Said to Supply 15% of U.S. Ecstasy Pills," *New York Times*, April 1, 2004.

Donald G. McNeil Jr., "Research on Ecstasy Is Clouded by Errors," *New York Times*, December 2, 2003.

Eric Nagourney, "Vital Signs: Consequences: Memory Often a Victim of Ecstasy," *New York Times*, April 10, 2001.

Carla Spartos, "Ecstasy Relieved from Agony," *Village Voice*, May 10, 2004.

——, "The Ecstasy Factor," *Village Voice*, March 10, 2004.

Dennis Wagner, "Gravano Faces a Grave Future," *Arizona Republic*, August 7, 2000.

——, "Gravano Partner Gives Damaging Testimony," *Arizona Republic*, May 5, 2002.

——, "Gravano Sentenced to 19-Year Term," *Arizona Republic*, October 31, 2002.

Internet Sources

ABC News, "Ecstasy: The New Cocaine?" abcnews.com, February 11, 2002. http://abclocal.go.com/wls/news/021102_ns_ecstasy.html.

Anonymous, "Dizziness, Panic Attacks, and Therapeutic Use." www.ecstasy.org/experiences/trip103.html.

Sheerly Avni, "Ecstasy Begets Empathy," Salon.com, September 12, 2002. www.salon.com/mwt/feature/2002/09/12/grob_interview/index.html.

Bangfrog, "Disintegration, Anxiety and Meltdown," Erowid.org. www.erowid.org/experiences/exp.php?ID=2445.

CBS, "The Heroin of the Heartland," cbsnews.com, July 31, 2002. www.cbsnews.com/stories/2002/01/31/health/main326497.shtml.

CBS, "Perfect Little Girl," *48 Hours*, cbsnews.com, July 26, 2001. www.cbsnews.com/stories/2000/11/28/48hours/main2528 11.shtml.

CNN, "'Ecstasy' Benefit?" *American Morning*, February 26, 2004. http://transcripts.cnn.com/TRANSCRIPTS/0402/26/ltm.19.html.

John Cloud, "The Lure of Ecstasy," *Time*, June 5, 2000. www.time.com/time/europe/magazine/2000/0717/cover.html.

DanceSafe, "What Is Ecstasy?" http://dancesafe.org/documents/druginfo/ecstasy.php.

Jonathan Darman, "Out of the Club, onto the Couch," *Newsweek*, December 5, 2003. www.maps.org/media/newsweekonline120503.html.

Kevin Durrheim, "Therapists on E," *New Therapist*. www.newtherapist.com/therape.html

Erowid, "Summary and Review of *Ecstasy Rising*, an ABC News report," Erowid.org, April 2004. www.erowid.org/chemicals/mdma/mdma_media1.shtml.

Arran Food, "Medicine Hope for Psychedelic Drugs," BBC News, August 15, 2004. http://news.bbc.co.uk/1/hi/health/3528730.stm.

Caleb Hellerman and Miriam Falco, "Ecstasy Approved for Medical Study," CNN.com, February 2, 2004. www.cnn.com/2004/HEALTH/02/25/ecstasy.study/index.html.

Karl Jansen, "Nocturnal Panic Attack," Ecstasy.org. http://ecstasy.org/qanda/q7.html.

King County, "Public Health Joined by Local and National Partners in Ecstasy Education Campaign," Public Health (Seattle and King County), February 14, 2002. www.metrokc.gov/HEALTH/news/02021401.htm.

Dawn MacKeen, "The Big E," Salon.com, July 7, 1999. www.dir.salon.com/health/feature/1999/07/07/ecstasy/index.html?sid=136202.

National Institute on Drug Abuse, "Long-Term Brain Injury From Use of Ecstasy." www.nida.nih.gov, www.nida.nih.gov/MedAdv/99/NR-614b.html.

Liz O'Brien, "The Agony After Ecstasy," Salon.com, June 14, 2000. http://dir.salon.com/health/feature/2000/06/14/ ecstasy/index.html?sid=836931.

Ted Oehmke, "The Poisoning of Suburbia," Salon.com, July 6, 2000. http://dir.salon.com/health/feature/2000/07/06/ pma/index.html.

———, "The War on Information," Salon.com, June 15, 2000. http://dir.salon.com/health/feature/2000/06/15/ecstasy_bill/index.html?sid=833331.

Office of National Drug Control Policy, "*Pulse Check* Trends in Drug Abuse Mid-Year 2000," *Pulse Check*. www.whitehouse drugpolicy.gov/publications/drugfact/pulsechk/midyear2000/ club drugs.html.

———, "Research Report Series —MDMA Abuse (Ecstasy)," National Institute on Drug Abuse. www.drugabuse.gov/Re searchReports/MDMA/ MDMA5.html#preventing.

PBS, "In the Mix: Ecstasy." www.pbs.org/inthemix/shows/ show_ecstasy.html.

Kristen Philipkoski, "Legal Ecstasy in Five Years?" Wired News, February 5, 2001. http://wired-vig.wired.com/news/tech nology/0,1282,41457,00.html.

Jessica Reaves, "The Pill That Has Parents in a Panic," *Time*, April 3, 2000. www.time.com/time/nation/article/0,8599,42405, 00.html.

Nicholas Saunders, "E for Ecstasy," Ecstasy.org, May 1993. www.ecstasy.org/books/e4x/.

Gerard Seenan, "Regular Ecstasy Users Risking Loss of Memory," *Guardian Unlimited*, March 29, 2001. http://society. guardian.co.uk/drugsandalcohol/story/0,8150,464981,00. html.

Jack Shafer, "Ecstasy Madness!" Slate.com, August 28, 2000. http://slate.com/id/1005971.

Mary Spicuzza, "Nightly Grind," *Metro*, March 23, 2000. www. metroactive.com/papers/metro/03.23.00/ecstasy1-0012.html.

Michele Spiess, "MDMA (Ecstasy)," Office of National Drug Control Policy, February 2004. www.whitehousedrugpolicy. gov/publications/factsht/mdma/index.html.

Gerald Valentine, "MDMA and Ecstasy," *Psychiatric Times*, February 2002. www.psychiatrictimes.com/p020246.html.

Benjamin Wallace-Wells, "The Agony of Ecstasy," *Washington Monthly*, May 2003. www.washingtonmonthly.com/features/2003/0305.wallace-wells.html.

Rick Weiss, "DEA Approves Trial Use of Ecstasy in Trauma Cases," *Washington Post*, March 2, 2004. www.maps.org/pipermail/maps_forum/2004-March/005984.html.

Bob Woodruff, "Ecstasy and Therapy," abcnews.com, April 1, 2004. www.abcnews.com/sections/WNT/Primetime/Ecstasy_therapy_040401.html.

Index

Picture Credits

About the Author

Stephanie Lane is a Wellesley graduate and a children's book editor living in New York City.